Solitary Tango

Viveca Tallgren

Solitary Tango

2019 © Viveca Tallgren
Front page picture: Viveca Tallgren
Cover: Larsen Lab
Printing: BoD – Norderstedt, Germany
ISBN: 978-87-9357-805-0

Contents

TO PARIS BY COUCHETTE COACH

Long before EasyJet, Ryanair and other low-cost airlines conquered the market, many Danes used to go by train to Paris. The journeys could be tough and Paris felt further away than today, where you can just go there by plane for a short shopping trip. Looking back, the hardships were also part of the charm. On the train, you had a feeling of literally being on a journey, and not least, the distance felt much longer. With my tight student budget I couldn't afford a sleeping car with a made bed and washbasin. I had to settle for the couchette coach with six plank beds for both sexes. You never knew what sort of passengers would come to sleep in the couchette on the way. On each plank bed there was a thin blanket, which offered no protection when the window was opened in the middle of the night due to bad smelling feet and other odours. The curtains were fluttering and, if you ended up with being on the upper bed without any bed guard with the wind blowing right in your face, you could forget all about getting a good night's sleep. The infernal rumbling of the train and some passengers' penetrating snoring also contributed to the sleepless night.

Early the next morning the ticket inspector knocked on the door and asked us all to leave the compartment, because he had to fold up the plank beds for seats. While the train drove through dreary Belgian factory areas, we were served café au lait with croissants as a foretaste of France. What a blessing it was when we finally caught a glimpse of Sacre Cæur and the Eiffel Tower in the distance. In those days, I was hardly an experienced traveller, and seeing these two buildings was like seeing one of the Seven Wonders of the World. Everything, even the miserable Parisian suburbs with their run-down houses, was seen in a flattering light as a part of the Parisian charm.

After the arrival at Gare du Nord I went down to the Metro with my recently acquired *carnet* and with my suitcase in tow, I continued through the long subterranean tunnels. There were not many elevators, but in return there was no lack of courteous gentlemen ready to help. Seeing the many nationalities and colours of skin gave me a sinking feeling, and all the chic women in tight skirts and high-heeled shoes made me feel boorish in my blue jeans. The rest of the afternoon was to be used for shopping for new clothes.

There were fuzz balls on the carpet in my hotel room, the lace curtains were faded by the sun and on the flowered wallpaper there was a reproduction of Renoir's *Bal du moulin de la Galette*

The pillow, at that time a constant feature in all French beds, consisted of a long cylindrical cushion on which your head was restlessly balancing giving quite a turbulent night's sleep. That was part of the charm, even if it has always puzzled me how the French have been able to sleep on such a monster.

After the long daily walking tours my lunch, a paper bag with pommes frites, was eaten on a bench in the Tuilerie Gardens by the fountain, where the kids were playing with their toy ships.

The idyll was suddenly interrupted by a male voice with an unmistakably Arabic accent. Did I enjoy my lunch in the lovely sunshine? He had a beautiful face with a slightly bowed nose, and eyes that were as dark as night.

Was I on holiday in Paris?

- *Oui.*

How did I like Paris?

- *Très bien.*

Should we have coffee together?

- *Non*, I have another appointment.

Just because you sit alone eating your lunch on a bench does not necessarily mean that you are accessible to any man. After another few attempts he gave up and almost aggressively turned his back and walked away.

A friend of mine had recommended that I contact the international organization People to People that facilitates contacts with local inhabitants. Eating at their house was meant to give you the opportunity to learn more about the local culture. I couldn't afford to experience the famous French gastronomy, but with People to People there was a possibility.

I looked at the list of hosts in Paris and my choice fell upon Madame Dumont, who lived on Boulevard Saint Michel. I imagined a typical Parisian attic flat with a view over the rooves and a little chic French woman who tripped around in a tight skirt and high-heeled shoes and invited me to enjoy the most delicious French specialities. Living on Boul Mich in the middle of the Latin Quarter couldn't be more French.

Before the visit to Madame Dumont, I tried on different clothes in front of the mirror and chose a chequered skirt and a red sweater. The new high-heeled shoes had to be replaced, though, by a pair of ballerinas; they had already given me some blisters on my toes during the long walks.

I took the elevator up to the fifth floor and took a last glance in the mirror before I rang the bell. After a short while, I heard the sound of quick steps. It didn't at all sound like high-heeled shoes. A chubby woman with curly hair and a chequered apron received me with a straightforward handshake.

- *Bonjour*, welcome to Paris. Is this your first visit to the city?

- No, I have been here twice before.

The apartment seemed somewhat untidy, as if she didn't have enough space. There were piles of books on the floor beside some cardboard boxes. And there in the corner of the living room I caught sight of the wheel chair with a severely disabled young man.

- *C'est mon fils Abel*, she said.

- *Abel, c'est Viveca de Danemark.* He rolled his eyes and tried to say something, and I hastened to say *bonjour*, hoping not to have to shake hands with him. I had never been so close to a disabled person. She took him into the small dining room where the table was set with a yellow tablecloth. In the middle, there were different pâtés, which didn't look very appetising. Was this really an example of the famous French gastronomy?

- Please, have a seat, she said and wheeled Abel to the table. She handed me the bread and asked if I had heard about *foie gras*.

- Yes, but I have never tasted it before.

She put a big piece of it on my plate. The sight of the brown mass was highly reminiscent of the film *Mondo Cane*, where a flock of geese were force-fed. The food was stuffed down in their long throats with a thick stick. Madame cut the food into pieces for Abel, who began to eat very noisily and spilled it on himself all the time. Madame wiped his mouth while she complained about the high prices of food and all the strikes and demonstrations in Paris. She talked continuously at a very fast pace, which challenged my understanding of the French, which I was studying at that time.

- You must taste my *pâté de champagne*. It is made after an old recipe of my mother's. She served the most delicious pâté de champagne, and I am trying the best I can to live up to her level. Our family and friends just loved it, she said while cutting a big piece of the heavy pâté for me.

- What does it contain? I asked trying to sound interested.

- Pork, chicken liver, onions, mushrooms, cream and a little cognac... Have some cor-

14

nichons with the pâté, she said, and handed me some of the small cucumbers.

I put a piece of the pâté in my mouth. The fat consistency made my stomach turn and I quickly put some cornichons in my mouth to counterbalance it.

- What have you seen in Paris? She asked while she put a large napkin around Abel's neck. She cut up a piece of pâté and put it in Abel's mouth and didn't seem very interested in hearing my answer.

- Notre Dame, the Louvre, Père Lachaise…

- Promise me you will see the Impressionists, and the Catacombs are also very interesting…, but why don't you eat anything? She exclaimed and looked at my plate with most of the foie gras left uneaten.

- I think I forgot to tell you that I am a vegetarian… I am so sorry about that…

- Never mind! she said, but I could feel her irritation.

- I'll make you a salad and meanwhile you two can talk to each other.

- You don't have to make it, I said, but she was already in the kitchen.

Abel was sitting opposite me. The large napkin that covered his shirt was filled with scraps of food. I smiled to him while his expressionless

15

eyes were looking at me. I looked down and pretended to be searching for something in my purse.

Madame came back with a small bowl with salad and a piece of cheese that I forced myself to eat even though I had already had lost my appetite.

The lunch was finished with coffee and petites fours in the living room. Madame began to tell me about her brother who was working in Cameroon. Her voice was frantic while she was telling about all the difficulties her brother was facing in Africa. She took a short pause to taste her petite four.

- I am sorry, I have to leave, I have to meet some friends.

I saw the disappointment in her eyes.

- Please excuse me for not telling you that I was a vegetarian…

- Don't think about it. I hope you liked the salad and the cheese.

A sudden feeling of guilt hit me when I went down in the elevator, and when I walked down Boulevard Saint Michel I was thinking about Madame Dumont's life alone with her disabled son. Had her husband left her because she had a disabled child, was he dead or had she just become pregnant by someone? I turned around

16

and looked up at the uppermost windows. What a destiny. But what was the benefit of the international cultural exchange that People to People advertised?

While I was looking through a newspaper at a café I caught sight of an advertisement for clairvoyance. This was before New Age became generally accepted and clairvoyance was still shrouded in mystique.

Marta Lewinsky lived in Montmartre. There was no elevator and, slightly breathless, I reached her door on the fourth floor. A middle-aged dark-haired woman dressed in a claret-coloured dress received me. With a heavy accent, she asked me to take a seat at a round table covered with a green tablecloth. From her accent, I guessed that she came from Eastern Europe or Russia.

- Where are you from? She asked me.

- From Finland, but I live in Denmark.

- What brings you to Paris?

- I like Paris very much.

On the table, there were several packs of cards, books about kabbalah and a crystal ball.

- Why have you come here? She asked.

- I found your advertisement in a newspaper and became curious… I want to know something about my future.

- Take the three uppermost cards from the pack and turn them over.

She looked at the card and began to look distant, as though she were in another world. When she came to herself again, she looked me in the eye.

- Are you in a relationship?

- Yes.

- You have bound yourself at an early age and you long to see the world, but right now you have to overcome some obstacles before your dream can come true. Maybe some economic problems. Maybe a separation, she said and looked me directly in the eye as if she was searching for a reaction. She closed her eyes as if she was consulting somebody.

- You are an individualist and you often feel other people to be a drag on you, she said and looked at me again with her serious eyes, which scared me a little. You will be travelling a lot and you prefer to travel alone. But you will always be divided between the necessity for security and family life on one hand and the necessity for travelling out into the unknown on the other.

She gathered the cards and looked at me again.

- In a ten years' time your life will change and you will enter a new phase with new challenges.

In a slightly heightened state of mind I returned to my hotel wondering if there was something about Marta Lewinsky's predictions or if it was all humbug.

On the way home to my hotel I ran into a poster with the text TANGO ARGENTIN. Under the text there was a photo of a couple; the woman had her hair put up in a knot and was dressed in a tight silk dress with a slit and a pair of high-heeled shoes, the man was in a black suit and his hair combed back with brilliantine. They stood in a very elegant and half erotic pose and the woman's leg was wound around the man's. To my great disappointment, I discovered that the tango show was the following evening when I would be sitting on the train back to Copenhagen.

Despite all my newfound inspiration, the journey home in the couchette coach was just as hard as the outward journey, when at least all the expectations of the legendary city could make the bad smell of sweaty socks and snoring sounds just a trivial matter. I shared the compartment with some Danes in foot-shaped shoes and floppy leisurewear, which was such a contrast to all the French esprit and elegance that I was so filled with now. Feeling superior to their boorish narrow outlook I picked the newest edition of the magazine Elle up from my handbag and began to read. That was long before my acquaintance with the play Jean de France by Ludvig Holberg at the Royal Theatre of Copenhagen. It's about a Danish young man, Hans, who had been in France and returned to Denmark as a puffed-up fool, who was feeling superior to his surroundings and thought that everything that was French was finer than the Danish.

THE RIDE TO COROICO

The queue in front of the ticket window was endless. A group of French tourists behind me were grumbling over the lack of efficiency. I had met them a few times on my journey through Bolivia and asked them for advice about some things, but when I met them again at the station in La Paz, they could barely say hello. Experienced globetrotters such as they would only reluctantly have a hopeless beginner such as me in tow.

While I was waiting, someone tapped me on the back. A tall and attractive guy with dark shoulder-length hair wanted to know if I could speak Spanish and could help him buy a ticket to Peru.

- Yes, of course.

It was quite a setback that the train for Peru didn't leave for two days, even if the timetable said the opposite.

- We could go together to Peru, he suggested, when at last we had got our tickets.

He was from New Zealand and was going on a hiking tour to Machu Pichu, the legendary Inca

23

citadel high up on a mountain top in the Andes. The thought of his lonely hiking tour in the Andes attracted me. I accepted.

In the background, I could hear the French tourists in discussion at the ticket window in quite poor Spanish. I felt a malicious pleasure at their difficulties.

- Do you have any plans for tomorrow? Sam asked.

- No, I had expected to go to Peru.

- Would you like to share a taxi to Coroico? It's a small town in Yungas, a tropical area about 50 kilometres from La Paz. The road is said to be fantastic.

Ignorant of what I had agreed to, I accepted his suggestion.

We walked together from the station to the Indian neighbourhood up the mountain slope. A labyrinth of stalls surrounded us, selling everything from vividly coloured spices to woven ponchos and knitted caps. All the inhabitants were almost a head or two shorter than us. They walked in a characteristic stride as if they were in a hurry. Some of the men were carrying heavy furniture on their backs and the women wore bowler hats and wide skirts and were spinning wool yarn on a small spinning wheel. On a small square people were crowding together. We drew nearer to see what was going on and caught sight of two black-haired women who were in the middle of a fight. On each side of them stood two grim men with folded arms looking at the two women as if they were watching a cockfight. The women were hissing, they were pitching into each other and pulling each other's hair, and then suddenly one of them stood with a big tuft of hair in her hand. I didn't want to see any more and we began to walk down towards the centre. Sam walked me to my hotel where we parted and went separate ways.

The next day we met at Plaza Murillo to find a taxi. Most of the drivers refused: "It's too far away", they said. A little worried by their refusals I thought of letting Sam go alone.

- It will be such a great experience, he assured me.

After several attempts, we finally found a driver who was willing to take us to Coroico and back but for a higher price. He wanted to go and tell his wife that he was leaving, and before he started the car, he made the Sign of the Cross.

- At first, we are going to drive through a high mountain pass before we begin the descent to Yungas, the driver explained.

The air got thinner and thinner, and when we reached the highest point, the ground was covered with a thin layer of snow. The car stopped at a small altar in the middle of the snow. It was misty and raw and the clouds were hanging so low that you felt you could touch them. The driver stepped out of the car and said that we could stretch our legs if we wanted to. He went to the small altar with a Virgin Mary and mumbled something while he knelt and made the Sign of the Cross. Afterwards, he stood for a short while in front of the altar and then he shouted *vámonos*.

We drove slowly down towards the more tropical areas, and about half an hour later a frighteningly beautiful mountain landscape opened before us. Steep green slopes were surrounding a canyon, which was so deep that you couldn't even see the bottom. The road continued along the mountainside, and on the opposite side, there was a steep precipice. It was a gravel road without any railings or room for overtaking, if two cars were to pass.

- Is this the road to Coroico? I asked. The driver confirmed it with stoic calmness.

I watched the light brown road, which twisted along the mountainside like a snake. It was too late to leave the car and return.

A little contrite, I had to admit my fear of mountain driving. Sam took my hand, but he seemed more interested in the mountain scenery than in me.

We approached a sharp curve. The road vanished from sight and it was as if we were driving straight down into the precipice. I closed my eyes and only the sound of the motor confirmed that we were still on the road. When I opened them again, there was the twisted road, which continued as far as the eye can see.

While we were driving, I caught sight of the small wooden crosses that popped up at regular intervals on the roadside.

- Why are there so many crosses? I asked the driver.

- They are on all the spots where a car fell down. If you drive downwards and meet another car, you have to overtake on the outermost side, and with the risk of falling down, but when you are driving upwards, you overtake on the innermost side, the driver told me with the same calmness as before, adding that this was the only place in Bolivia, where they keep to the left.

I could feel the sweat pouring down my arms. A story by Miguel Ángel Asturias came to my mind. A bus driver was taking a group of American tourists into the mountains of Guatemala.

His repressed hatred of Americans invoked his desire to frighten the passengers with some rash driving that ultimately made the bus plummet down the mountainside with all the passengers on board. I imagined how our taxi might lose balance upon overtaking and rolled down the mountainside. I saw myself sitting there with the certainty of heading for death. What about my kids at home? My two little girls... I hadn't been able to phone them because the telephone lines were so bad in Bolivia. The lump in my throat grew bigger and I was struggling to hold back my tears. I folded my hands under my bag and said a quiet prayer in my mind – the same way that I did when I was afraid as a child. Was this a punishment? It began with a small advertisement on the noticeboard at the university by a new French travel agency with fabulous prices on flights to South America. But Christian had also been in Tanzania while I took care of the kids. "How exciting!" all our friends said and asked if they could come and see his slides when he was back again. I never got that backing when I had booked my journey to South America. "Are you travelling alone?" "What about the kids?", "Why don't you travel together?" they asked in the middle of a progressive decade with constant debates on the existing family norms and when the feminists were defending equal rights for both sexes. Barely had I left, before Christian's mother moved into our apartment to help him take care of the kids.

I was interrupted by the car that was slowly approaching us.

- Are we going to overtake that car?

- Yes, answered the driver.

- I don't want to sit in the car while you are overtaking.

- As you wish.

When the oncoming car was about five metres from us, I ran out and pressed myself to the mountain wall. The car drove very close to the mountain, and the driver shouted to me to go forward. The two cars passed each other with difficulty. The driver, visibly irritated, asked me to get back into the car. Sam, on the contrary, seemed totally unaffected.

The air became warmer the further down we came into the valley and the vegetation became fertile.

- If I can't pass that puddle, you'll have to get out and push, the driver said and pointed at a small stream of water that ran into the road and made it muddy.

- Is there a risk of us slipping?

- In the worst case, yes.

We got out to push, but the driver managed the obstacle.

Down in the valley the vegetation became more and more fertile, with palm trees and tropical plants, and high above us the road twisted like a diabolical serpent. The driver stopped the car in front of a bar.

- I'll give you an hour's break in Coroico. We have to go back before sunset, the driver said.

The rhythmic calypso music made the dark and gloomy bar a little more colourful. In a corner two men were drinking beer.

- What do you want? Sam asked.

- Just a beer... I can't eat anything after that ride.

- But on the way back we are going to drive on the innermost side he said, and winked at me. I discovered the dark wet blotches on my t-shirt and put the jacket over my shoulders to hide them.

The waiter approached our table with slow steps, and with an indolent expression on his face, he took a note of our order.

- Didn't you know at all what you persuaded me into?

- It wasn't that bad, was it?

- Don't tell me that this road isn't dangerous.

- He is a very skilled driver and he knows this road very well.

The waiter came with our beers and a sandwich for Sam. I took a few sips of my beer and slowly recovered again. Sam told me about his lonely hikes in New Zealand, Norway and Switzerland.

- Why do you hike alone? I asked.

- I don't know… I haven't found anyone who wants the same things as I want… I am a lonely traveller … What about yourself? You also travel alone, don't you?

- Actually, it is the first time I've travelled this far…

- How do you like it?

- Exciting… especially the feeling of being totally independent of anyone…

- Then you probably don't want my company on the way to Peru.

- Yes, I want to go with you.

- We were interrupted by the driver, who shouted that we had to go.

- Now you don't have to get out if we meet other cars on the way, the driver said. It was the first time I saw him smile.

One evening many years later, I found the road to Coroico on the Internet. *El camino de la muerte,*

"The Death Road", it is called today and is said to be the most dangerous road in the world. There were photos of people who were cycling on it. The diabolical road had apparently become a target for the many practitioners of extreme sports.

I also found Sam on Facebook. He had become grey-haired and close-cropped and looked like any middle-aged man. I typed a message to him and asked if he still remembered our ride to Coroico and the nightly sail in moonlight over the Titicaca Lake. *Yes of course!* He promptly answered and sent me a friend request. There were many photos on his Facebook page of mountain hikes in groups with his wife and their friends. But he was not any longer the lonely rider who persuaded me to go with him on that breakneck drive.

THE HOTEL ROOM IN
VILLAHERMOSA

I chose to make a stop in a city with the melodious name Villahermosa, the beautiful town, in the Mexican state of Tabasco. After a twelve-hour drive in a bus with rattling windows and uncomfortable seats, I made an exception and paid for a good hotel. It was in the middle of my student years and I couldn't afford any luxury. Accommodation, food and transport were Spartan.

What a great feeling to enter a big hotel room with a broad double bed which reminded me of a bridal couch. After having lived in cheap hostels with a bathroom in the yard and a shower which often only produced a stream of water so thin that it couldn't wash out the soap from my hair, it was a sheer luxury to walk into the large bathroom with a bathtub and a washbasin with gilded taps. I was just about to wash my sweaty face in the washbasin, when I saw the beast: a four-centimetre long cockroach, which was sitting beside the soap on the washbasin twitching its long antennae. I ran out of the bathroom and rolled up a newspaper to kill the invader with it, but it had apparently smelled a rat and had disappeared. Never before had I seen a cockroach of that size.

In the late afternoon, the town seemed to have gone to sleep because of the suffocating humidity. On the benches in the shadow of the trees men were sleeping or sitting on the pavement staring blankly at thin air. This city was not accustomed to tourists and did not at all live up to its beautiful name. I met gaping faces everywhere, the children considered me a being from Jurassic Park, and to walk around in Mexico, a macho country par excellence, with blond hair was often a bit of a trial. I had to get away from there as fast as possible. I walked down to the bus station and bought a ticket to San Bartolomé de las Casas the next day. With the ticket in my bag I went to one of the cheap restaurants to have some tortillas with frijoles, mashed kidney beans, and a beer.

The rest of the evening I spent in the bridal couch reading a newly bought illustrated book about torture methods in the South American dictatorships. It was at the end of the 70s when a significant part of the South American continent was governed by anti-communist military dictatorships, which had begun a brutal policy of persecutions and torture of leftists. The book was to be read before I reached Central America, where you could be at risk if the border police found compromising literature in your luggage. On the front page, there was a picture of a naked woman whose hands and feet were tied to a pole from which she was hanging with her head downwards with an expression of horror in her eyes. The descriptions of what these regimes were capable of inflicting on their opponents, surpassed my fantasy.

At the University of Copenhagen there were often protest actions against the repression in Latin America, and support groups were created in solidarity with the political prisoners. The hallways were full of posters from different leftist factions about the topic and there were frequent meetings with speeches by the Chilean refugees, who received the status of brave guerrillas. Contrasts often attract each other. Many of the dark-haired female partners who accompanied the male refugees were exchanged for blonde Danish women with blue eyes, who showed their solidarity with the action against the dictatorships, sometimes with great family tragedies as a result. I had the feeling of being in a vacuum. To avoid being totally outside the discourse, I sporadically participated in the meetings, where I always felt like a stranger. You

had to prepare manifestos against the dictatorships in South America, distribute propaganda
material in the street and similar actions which I
tried to avoid with all sorts of excuses for not
participating. I liked to read poems by García
Lorca and Juan Ramón Jiménez and sometimes I
even read women's magazines in secret. But to
write an extended essay about poetry was not
considered politically relevant, and my choice
fell on the repression on Indians in Peru. Not
because there was anything wrong with the subject, but from a scientific point of view the thesis
is a potential investigative project which ideally
requires full engagement from the student so
that he or she can contribute something new and
original. My extended essay was original, by
focusing on the poet Cesar Vallejo's almost completely unexplored prose. However, my choice
was dictated by the prevailing culture at that
time. While writing it, my ex-husband gave me
the surname "Marx". He truly enjoyed provok-
ing leftists, claiming that he was a right-wing
supporter when the political discussions became
too dogmatic.

While I was lying there in the bridal couch
with my torture book, and feeling more and
more shocked about what human beings are
capable of doing, I ended up throwing the book

into the waste basket. Nonetheless, the awareness of having the book with all its monstrosities in the room, made it difficult for me to fall asleep.

I woke up in the middle of the night bathed in sweat and turned the light on to find my bottle of water. In that very moment, I saw swarms of black cockroaches that hurried to the nearest crack in the floor and I could hear the rattling sound of their legs on the tiles. On the bedhead of my bridal coach there was a little caravan and down in the wastebasket, where the torture book was lying next to half a packet of biscuits, the black beasts were swarming. I was told that they feed on corn. I took out my spray deodorant and sprayed it into the wastebasket several times, which made them interrupt their meal and hurry to the nearest crack or shadow. The rest of the night I lay on the bed with the light turned on. As soon as I closed my eyes, I saw the swarms of black cockroaches running over the floor and onto my bedhead.

Apparently, there is a reason why the evocative rhythmic song *La cucaracha* – The cockroach – has almost become a national song in Mexico.

SPECIAL PRICE FOR YOU

I don't like party tours but, at the thought of walking alone in a Moroccan city, I began to consider a guided bus tour to Tetouan arranged by a Danish agency. The stories about the white slave trade suddenly became menacingly alive. And, as my husband said on the phone: You might also learn something when travelling in a group. After all, it's only a day!

The bus for Algeciras left at seven o'clock in the morning from a big hotel in Torremolinos. The guide, Pedro, who was standing in a white t-shirt with the logo of the Danish agency Spies over his chest, welcomed us in Danish with a heavy Spanish accent.

I took advantage of the waiting time in Algeciras, before we went on board, to walk around at the port, which gave me a foretaste of what to expect on the other side of the Strait of Gibraltar. A large ferry was about to leave for Tangier. The cars, which were loaded to bursting point with mattresses, baby carriages and other luggage tied on the roof, began to drive on board.

In one of the shops you could buy honey in enormous jars. The queue reached far out into the street. At the counter an elderly man with an embroidered skullcap was discussing the price with the seller, who refused to lower it, but the man did not give up. His Arabic accent made the tone of his voice sound even more insistent. He WANTED to lower the price, even if the seller kept saying NO! Behind him there were several men in skullcaps, who also wanted to hoard honey for the journey back home, and the queue grew even longer.

Pedro was waving to us. We were to go on board the hydrofoil. One by one we sat down in front of an enormous screen, which was showing a dramatic love story. The motor started and soon the waves sprayed the windows. The film reached its climax as the Rock of Gibraltar rock passed by the windows. The principal male character, beside himself with jealousy, hit his woman, who collapsed in tears on the floor with a bleeding nose accompanied by boisterous music, which drowned the room.

Soon the North African coastline emerged with the Rif Mountains in the background, and shortly afterwards the boat stopped at Ceuta, where a bus was waiting for us. We climbed on board, and Pedro pointed out to us that we were not yet in Morocco, because Ceuta is a Spanish enclave.

At the Spanish-Moroccan border outside Ceuta there was an endless queue of tired and exhausted people, who were waiting to get into Spain. Because of the illusion of a better life in the EU, they are prepared to offer anything. Pedro chatted with the frontier guards and patted them amicably on the shoulders. They took an indifferent glance at the bus and then we drove along.

- Welcome to Morocco, which is a Muslim country... Morocco is also part of the Maghreb and is ruled by King Hassan, who is beloved by his fellow countrymen.

- What is Maghreb? One of the passengers asked.

- It is a term for Morocco, Tunisia, Algeria, Western Sahara and Mauretania, Pedro answered. – Moroccans love good food and they also like tubby women, he added, while squinting at a well-built woman on the bus.

Men in round skull caps and long woven coats were walking on the road, and behind the mud-built houses slender minarets rose in the background.

The bus stopped in the middle of a barren plain, where a flock of camel drivers were waiting with their bleating camels.

- You are going to ride a camel! Pedro shouted enthusiastically.

The camel driver, who didn't look very friendly at all, signalled each of us to sit down on a camel. Barely had I sat down, before I heard the crack of the whip and the camel got up with a jerk. A boy with a colourful skullcap and shabby trousers was ready with his camera and took pictures of me while the camel walked a short round trip. Another crack was heard and the camel lay down again. With the same unfriendly look the camel driver again signalled me to get off and then he showed me a small note: "$5 for ride and photo".

- You bloody bastards are not going to get anything! We are not going to pay a penny! A short-haired woman shouted. She and her husband went directly into the bus. Their camel driver shouted something in Arabic to his colleague and waved the whip around and the air was filled with the coarse sounds of their language. I quickly paid him and hurried into the bus.

- How brash! We haven't even asked for that ride and least of all to be photographed! The woman shouted to Pedro, while her husband was sulking beside her.

- It's part of the programme, Pedro explained.

- Five dollars won't ruin you. After all, we are far better off than they are, I shouted.

- Mind your own business! The woman hissed.

- We are approaching Tetouan, where we are going to have lunch in a Moroccan home, Pedro said.

We drove into the city and the bus stopped in front of a residential property.

A man dressed in a beige suit was standing at the entrance and welcomed us. The stairway, which was decorated on both sides with beautiful blue and white tiles, led up to a big salon with pillars, finely ornamented panels and oriental carpets on the floor. Straight out of the Arabian Nights.

Pedro explained the menu, which consisted of rabbit soup, couscous with camel meat on a spit, yoghurt with honey and, to finish, mint tea with a selection of Moroccan pastry. I would have preferred to sit alone, but I felt that it was too anti-social. I cast a sidelong glance at the other tables, but didn't sense any interest from the other participants. At last I screwed up my courage and asked an elderly couple if they would mind if I sat at their table.

- No, not at all, don't you agree, Ejnar? The woman said.

- No, please have a seat, her husband added.

The food was served by servants dressed in white cotton suits, and when we began to eat, two Berber musicians in brightly coloured costumes came in and began to play and sing lively rhythmic songs with melancholy undertones. The couple I shared a table with looked disapprovingly at the food without touching it.

- I have some biscuits and bananas in the bag, the woman whispered to her husband.

Pedro clapped his hands.

- After lunch, you are going for a walk with Ali, our local guide, in the medina, the old fortified part of Tetouan. It is surrounded by a wall with seven gates.

The two Berbers stopped playing and placed themselves at the exit with their hats in their hands. Some of the Danes went out without paying any attention to the musicians, whose formerly smiling faces suddenly shifted to a gruff expression. I quickly put a few coins in their hat, but I didn't even get a thank you in return.

Ali, a tall and imposing man in a long brown coat and skullcap was waiting in the street. We followed him and walked through the onion-shaped gate Bab er Rouah. It was like entering in the Middle Ages. We walked in a single file through the narrow alleys with all sorts of booths and workshops. It reminded me of my primary school in Helsinki where, after each break, we also walked in a single file up to our classrooms.

In the Moroccan bazaar, everything was done manually. At the tailor's shop they used a sewing machine with pedals, and the shoemaker was hammering away with an old hammer. The two young girls in front of me were dressed in low-cut sun tops, with bare midriffs and white shorts. They were talking about previous night at a discotheque in Torremolinos and hardly noticed the looks of the passers-by. An old man stopped and with an aggressive movement he placed his stick on the ground, while staring at them.

With a hand movement Ali asked us to make room for a herd of goats. A herdsman hustled them with his stick and, frightened, some of them produced a stream of droppings that looked like small round liquorice pastilles onto the cobblestones.

Suddenly the muezzin's voice resounded over the small alleys. We passed a mosque and through the half-open door you could catch a glimpse of the prayer mats on the floor between the white pillars. One of the men immediately turned his video camera on and tiptoed to the door to film. *No picture! No picture!* Ali shouted and gesticulated with his fist, while the man with the camera returned with an almost offended expression.

We were taken to a carpet shop, where five sellers were standing ready to welcome us. Hardly had we entered before the selling procedure began. *Lady, look, very nice, very nice!* Their whispering voices said everywhere. One carpet after another, each more beautiful than the other, were spread out in front of us. Carpets with geometrical patterns in red, blue and ochre shades. *Special price for you. Very cheap, very cheap,* the man next to me insisted. He didn't even react to my repeated *No thank you* but just kept spreading the carpets while repeating *Lady, look, very nice, very nice.*

After half an hour Ali clapped his hands as a sign that we were to leave the shop. Barely had we entered the street before a herd of bag sellers rushed towards us. I pushed one of the most insistent away and, in return, I got a hard slap on my arm with one of the bags that were hanging on his arm. Ali, who was waiting a little further away, behaved as if nothing had happened, but his malicious smile was unmistakable.

We entered a true labyrinth of small alleys, where they were selling all sorts of exotic goods along the pavements: woven fabrics, basket works, spices in all the colours of the rainbow, Moroccan slippers, and so on. At a little square where shiny vases, bowls and plates of bronze were spread out on the ground, Ali stopped and turned around. "Now I have a surprise for you!", he exclaimed with a secretive smile. As if a magic incantation had been uttered, a short man with dark sunglasses, a white coat and two small suitcases in each hand appeared. He bowed to us, opened one of the suitcases and took out a long black snake, which twisted around his neck. With the snake in his hand he went to a blond guy from the group and let it slip down in his shirt. *Not dangerous! No poison! h*e assured. The guy was laughing hysterically while beads of sweat appeared on his sunburnt forehead. The snake charmer took up the snake and put it back in the suitcase and took a smaller shiny light brown snake from the other suitcase. It showed its oscillating tongue and the snake charmer gave it a kiss. I hid behind the others when he got nearer with the snake in his hand. *Mama try snake!* he said to a chubby woman with short red hair. She cheerfully took hold of the snake and let it twist around her neck and her arms. *Very good, mama, very good!* He shouted and put the snake back in the suitcase. Finally, he took a piece of red cloth up from his pocket and unfolded it into a small bag and passed it to the whole group to collect money. A moment after he had disappeared in the crowd just as suddenly as he had appeared.

We followed Ali, who walked through the crowd and the endless labyrinth of alleys and stalls with domestic utensils, leather goods, basket works, dried fruit, nuts and other dainties. The mere thought of getting lost here made me toe the line and keep to the herd.

Pedro was waiting at the bus outside the medina and we drove back to the hydrofoil boat. Before the crossing, we stopped at the parking place in Ceuta in front of two enormous super markets.

- Does anyone want to buy duty-free goods? Ceuta is a duty-free area. Almost everybody put up their hands.

We were given half an hour to shop. Everybody rushed into the super market and began to fill the trollies. Half an hour later people came out dragging big bags filled with cigarettes, chocolate, liquorice allsorts and spirits.

The sun was about to set and it was starting to get dark when we sailed back to Algeciras. Behind us Ceuta was glittering like a diamond with the Rif Mountains in the background.

When we reached Algeciras Port, the shop with the honey jars was closed and everything was quiet and empty. We got into the bus that was to take us back to Torremolinos. I took one of the front seats. Behind me I heard my fellow passengers' vigorous chatting. It was as if the relief of being back in Europe had produced a more unrestrained atmosphere. I looked out of the window. A thin dog was sniffing around and cocked its leg against a lamppost. It looked confused and lonely. I sympathised with it.

THE PASSION OF SILENCE

Could this Finnish provincial one-horse town really be the leading tango town in the world after Buenos Aires? The station at Sienäjoki was inanimate and deserted, and I asked myself if I had got off at the wrong place.

To be sure, I asked a man at the station if there was to be a tango festival here. *Sinne päin* he mumbled without batting an eyelid and pointed to what had to be the centre of the town. While I passed the rows of modern concrete houses, each more depressing than the last, I heard the melancholy tones of a well-known Finnish tango in the distance. When I came nearer, I could see an enormous signpost with the text TANGOKATU, the tango street. At the entrance to the closed street there were a few couples who were swinging back and forth, keeping pace with the music. Every now and then a man bent his woman over so that her long hair almost touched the ground. The men were determinedly leading their women, but the choreography was not as sophisticated as in the Argentine tango, which I had seen in a few films and read some books about.

At last I found the house where I was to rent a room. The few hotels of the town had long ago been booked up. A tall blond man welcomed me and showed me to my room. There was a bed, a table of artificial wood, a yellow armchair and a bookcase. The view of the wood with pines, spruces and birches counterbalanced the dull furnishings. He gave me a couple of towels, a key for the house and the most essential practical information before he left. He was as taciturn as the protagonists in Aki Kaurismäki's films.

At the caravan site nearby, hundreds of guests from all over Finland were making their arrangements with garden furniture, picnic baskets and outdoor grills. In the centre of the town they were playing tango music in the only department store in the town, where the vestibule was filled with dancing couples. Unlike the Argentine tango dancers' strict elegance, the Finns were dressed in anything from sneakers and jogging bottoms to floral summer dresses, high-heeled shoes and dark suits, even rubber boots were seen on the dance floor. Fat and thin, young and old, everybody was tramping enthusiastically in step with the tango music.

Quite near the Tango Street I caught sight of the signpost "Åke Blomqvist's dancing school". Blomqvist was my childhood dancing teacher in Helsinki! Even if he was now an elderly man, he was still active. For more than a generation Blomqvist was Finland's most popular dancing teacher. I presented myself as his former pupil and asked if I could ask him a few questions about the tango. He smiled archly and anticipated me. "The women are too educated today to follow the man, and the men have become too wimpy to lead the self-willed women," he whispered to me and clapped his hands to make the couples keep the pace. My visit was inopportune in the middle of the dance lesson, and I had to say goodbye. He winked at me and went on clapping.[1]

The Tango Street was surrounded by stalls selling Carelian pirogues, different kinds of smoked fish, sausages and sandwiches made from rye bread. Alko, the Finnish alcohol monopoly, had their own stand, and there was plenty of it to wash away any possible inhibitions. Why can a Finnish man barely offer a compliment to a woman, unless he has consumed at least five whiskeys, while Italian men can, with-

---

[1] Åke Blomqvist died in 2013, aged 88.

out a pause, shower women with flattering adjectives, each one more adulatory than the last?

Totally fascinated, I was watching the dancing couples, when somebody tapped me on the shoulder. A heavily built man with crew-cut blond hair and moustache asked me if I wanted to dance.

- I don't know if I can... I haven't learned it, I said.

- It's not difficult, he answered curtly.

I went with him to the dance floor. We stepped in time with the music. With Åke Blomqvist's remark about the self-willed women in mind I let him lead me, but several times I bumped into his feet.

- Sorry.

- It's okay, he said and a strong smell of alcohol touched my nostrils.

- Are you a Swedish-speaking Finn? He asked.

- Yes. Why?

- You made a couple of errors in your Finnish...

I felt more and more hopeless on the dance floor and imagined that his leading was getting worse because he knew that I was a Swedish-speaking Finn.

- Could we take a break? I asked when the music stopped playing.

- Okay. As you want, he said and shrugged his shoulders without saying another word.

With a lump in my throat I returned to my room. The sun had set, but the night was still young.

There are Finns who have a grudge against the Swedish-speaking minority, and vice versa. It has a historical explanation. From the Middle Ages until 1809 Finland belonged to Sweden, and for long after Swedish was the language of the elite. Today, the Swedish-speaking Finns are only a small minority of 5% of the population, but the cultural differences between the two language groups are still perceptible. The Swedish-speaking author, Kjell Westö, has described the richness it is to be bilingual – for better or worse in his article "To live with two languages under your skin". It is like changing identity when you alternate between your Swedish mother tongue and Finnish, he explains, but he also admits that he never would write a novel in Finnish, because there are more nuances in the mother tongue.

Even though I have lived in Denmark for many years and hold Danish citizenship, it still makes me extremely sad knowing that there are Finns who still wish the Swedish minority were far away. But what do they get out of eliminating all the traces of a cultural heritage, which is felt to be uncomfortable?

The culmination of the Seinäjoki festival was the election of the tango queen and king. The contest took place under great festivity, a kind of a Finnish grand prix contest. The female and male finalists danced separately with a selected tango piece in the neon-illuminated scene, the women in long low-necked ball gowns with tinsel and shining sequins, and the men in dark suits and brilliantine in their hair accompanied by an orchestra all dressed entirely in white. The chosen tango queen and king each received a golden crown each on their heads and, for the rest of the summer, their songs were heard in the buses, cafés and the dancing pavilions at the lakeside. A unique piece of Finnish popular culture, both clumsy and poetic in a fabulous mixture. Rubber boots and ballroom dresses with shining sequins combined with to the tones of beautiful sentimental songs about longings and love. It couldn't be more Finnish.

The final ball in the sports centre was celebrated with the tango queen and king and all the finalists, who entertained the audience with one melancholy song after another. I was sitting among the wallflowers watching the dancing couples who moved closer and closer to each other under the twinkling neon lights. The women closed their eyes with a dreamy expression while they were led by their serious-looking men. There was also my coarse-cut dancing partner with a young brunette in a red silk dress, whom he bent against the floor and then continued with rhythmic steps along the floor.

The day after all the caravans left Seinäjoki, and soon everything was as stone-dead as before. While I was looking at the endless woods in the train back to Helsinki I remembered the words of my girlfriend, a Swedish-speaking Finn, before I left for Seinäjoki:

"To Seinäjoki! ... The tango festival! ... That is a brave thing to do!

ON THE WAY TO PLAZA ITALIA

I like to observe people, but my daughter has often reproached me for staring too indiscreetly.

Newly arrived in Buenos Aires, I went out to explore the centre of the city. On Avenida 9 de Julio, reportedly the widest street of the world, and close to the unmistakable obelisk, I caught sight of an exceptionally attractive guy with dark curly hair and trimmed stubble. My surprise was immense when, shortly after, someone tapped me on the shoulder.

- Want to talk? The attractive guy, at whom I had just looked, asked.

- Why? I asked, totally staggered, while looking at his dark eyes.

For heaven's sake, I didn't mean it like that, I thought in my ignorance about the norms and values of this city. Soon I discovered, though, that the looks have a different signal value here than in Northern Europe, where you can look as much as you want at a man without anything happening.

While I was roaming the streets in the centre, I saw a woman with magnificent black hair flow-ing down her shoulders. She was sitting in a café observing the passers-by. Suddenly her eyes caught sight of an elderly grey-haired man in a dark blue coat and hat, who was walking in front of me. Immediately, she began to act coquettishly and initiated a seductive and almost impudent temptation. The elderly man stopped for a moment, turned back, and went back into the café. Totally fascinated by this wordless communication between two strangers, I followed the man into the café. He went to the woman's table and said something to her, while her eyes were playing invitingly. He sat down at her table with his back to me. There were no free tables near them, so I had to content myself with the last row. He ordered an aperitif for them both, and they exchanged a few words with each other. From time to time, she insinuatingly slipped her fingers through her thick dark hair. When they had drunk their aperitifs and he had paid the bill, they got up and walked towards the entrance. I wanted to follow them, but the waiter was busy. When I finally got a chance to pay, they were already gone.

Now I also wanted to become acquainted with the Argentine tango and was invited by a good friend to a so-called *práctica*, where you could receive training in the many codes that had to be observed at the dancing salons of the city, such as, for example, to ask for a dance with your eyes. We were ten in all, five men and five women. First, we all changed shoes in the entrance hall. The four other women, who were all Argentine, put on their dancing shoes with high pointed heels, while they all were talking at once about their respective personal problems. I followed them into the small room, and we sat down on a bench in one end of the room, while the five men went to the opposite end. When the music began to play, the men chose a female dancing partner, whom they invited with the eyes and slight inclination of the head. With a discreet smile the women expressed their acceptance and met their partner on the dance floor. If a woman does not want to dance with a man in the tango salons, her look will be slightly nonplussed, when she declines the unwanted invitation. She will turn her head away in another direction and pretend that she hasn't seen the invitation. The man can, of course, go to her table and ask her to dance, but the more anonymous exchange of looks is preferred to avoid any potentially embarrassing situations. According to the rules, it is considered disrespectful to refuse an invitation. It is a question of finding the right but subtle balance between the respectable and the disreputable.

I caught a look and signalled my acceptance of the invitation as well as I could, with a discreet smile my acceptance of the invitation. The man was American and had settled in Buenos Aires to learn tango.

- Oh my, it sure is a difficult dance!

He had an evident need to talk and broke all the rules about silence during the dance. I followed him as well as I could and wished that he would stop talking. After the third dance, we sat down and a new round started. One of the men, an Asian, looked in my direction and I answered his invitation. I did my utmost to listen to the music and the heartrending song about a man who had been abandoned by his woman. His leading was simple and the small breaks he took in the middle of the dance felt like pauses in the middle of an exciting story. After the three obligatory rounds, he asked if I wanted to try a real *milonga*.

We met with some of his friends at the dancing salon *El Beso*. Here the looks fluttered through the room and created a special energy in the place. Frank, timid and secretive looks that contributed to the electric tension in the crowded dancing room. By a coincidence, I met a Danish woman who had spent a fortune on journeys to Buenos Aires and private lessons with the leading tango dancers in the city. There was something funny and almost adolescent about her devotion to the dance. "It's the tenth time I've visited Buenos Aires", she said and confided to me that she was 58. She considered leaving her job and her boyfriend, who didn't like to dance tango, and settle in the Argentine capital.

- I know the city as well as if it were my native town, she said, but we didn't speak further, because, without my discovering more, she was asked to dance.

She put her arm at an angle over her partner's shoulder, closed her eyes and let herself be led over the dancing floor in her red dress and matching shoes.

But what is it that attracts us women to the Argentine capital? The draw is hardly the tango alone but rather, perhaps, all the piquancy that takes place in almost every corner of the city.

Down in Buenos Aires' subway I caught sight of a man who reminded me of the author Julio Cortázar. Suddenly he looked up and our eyes met for a brief instant. Shortly after he got up and moved on towards the exit where I was standing, but I lost sight of him in the crowd. I had learned from my experience that I shouldn't turn around and look after him. At the next station, I heard someone whisper something just behind me. It sounded like *encantadora*, enchanting. I looked around and saw "Julio Cortázar", who hurried out and disappeared in the crowd on the platform.

When I got off at Plaza Italia, I discovered that my bag had been opened. My wallet was gone.

THE BEACH OF
PONDICHERRY

There was nothing disturbing about the deserted beach of Pondicherry when the sun was setting in the Bay of Bengal. I let my feet sink down into the warm sand and enjoyed the empty beach and the sea, when suddenly I heard children's voices behind me. Three happy-looking children, a girl of about eight years with wispy hair and two smaller boys came running towards me. They said something that I didn't understand. I tried in different ways by means of mime and gesticulations to explain that I didn't understand their language. They laughed and I laughed, too, but suddenly they began to tear at my bag. They pulled with a frightening power and nobody else was on the beach. I looked them in their eyes. *Stop it! Stop it!* I shouted. But there was something diabolical in their eyes, so far from my idea about children as innocent beings. I pushed them, I threatened them with my fist and shouted: *You bloody bitches!* at them, but it was all in vain. *That's enough! Go to hell!* I shouted as loud as I could and was about to give the aggressive girl a slap in her face, when they suddenly released my bag and ran away. With slightly shaky legs I tried to recuperate and to continue my walk back to the hotel. I stopped several times to make sure that the kids had not come back.

The beach was still deserted and the only person I could see, was a man, who was lying a little further away at the water's edge. What a funny place to sleep, I thought, but he might have drunk too much. The feeling of approaching a human being was, after all, reassuring.

As I came nearer the man, it was as if he was lying so still. I slowly approached him and suddenly I saw the big cut across his neck. I stood there looking at him, totally paralysed. A murdered man!

In the distance, I saw a thin man walking in my direction. He was dressed in a "dhoti", the small loincloth, such as Gandhi also wore.

- There is a dead man! There is a dead man! I shouted and pointed at the murdered man.

The man continued his walk as if nothing had happened and just shrugged his shoulders.

My original attraction to India, which had brought me here for a second time, disappeared. I only saw cynicism and indifference everywhere. There were too many people. Human lives didn't have any meaning at all. They had a down-to-earth relation to death. The dead were

76

carried on a bier in the streets to the fire, which would send them to the eternal circuit, accompanied by drums and music. *Moksha,* the release from the endless series of incarnations was the goal for every Hindu for whom death was the most important event in life. What was it that was so attractive in this country?

When I came back to the hotel I breathlessly informed the receptionist that there was a dead man at the edge of the water. He looked up with a tired expression, which clearly confirmed that he had more important things to do. He promised to do something about it, but that was a lie.

- Now, I suggest that you don't think any more about this. I suggest that you should go to our beautiful dining room and enjoy our fantastic buffet. We have the best Indian food in town.

COME TO SANTIAGO, THAT'S WHERE THE ACTION IS!

I had come by train to the city of León, where I was to participate in a course. When I found my boarding house the entrance was blocked by three bicycles. I was just about to leave and find another place to stay at when the three owners of the bikes came running and apologized several times while they removed their vehicles.

In the evening, I ate at a restaurant called El Peregrino, the Pilgrim, just beside the cathedral. Someone was waving to me from another table. It was one of the three owners of the bikes. He came to my table and presented himself and asked if I would like to sit with him and his two friends.

The three guys were pals from university and lived in different parts of Spain, and each summer they met in Barcelona and went on a cycling tour along the Pilgrim's route to Santiago de Compostela. Previously, they had walked on foot and spent the nights at pilgrim's hostels, but now that they all had their families, they chose to cycle to save time. If you were a real pilgrim, you could only walk on foot or cycle, they said. The best thing about the tour was the sense of community and solidarity among the people you met on your way. In unison, they kept telling me about how your senses become awakened during the walk and about all the fragrances and sounds of nature of which you suddenly become aware.

- Promise us you will make that walk, they said before our paths separated.

- I will, I assured them.

After the meeting with the cyclists, I threw myself into anything I could find about the Pilgrim's Road to Santiago. About how it came into existence in the Middle Ages during the Christian conquest of Spain by the Arabs. About the ferocious story about James the Apostle alias Santiago, who was beheaded in Jerusalem and whose bodily remains, according to the legend, were sailed to Spain by his disciples, who buried him on the place where Santiago de Compostela Cathedral stands today.

I decided to see Santiago de Compostela in connection with the 2004 Holy Year of Saint James – a tradition that has its origin in the 12th century, when the Pope prescribed that those who visited the Cathedral during the Sunday celebration of the Day of Saint James were absolved. Since that time, the Spaniards have celebrated the Holy Year of Saint James when the 25th of July falls on a Sunday.

Regardless of all the beautiful stories about the *Camino*, as it is popularly called, I didn't keep my promise to the three cyclists. The mere thought of blisters, sore feet and communal overnight stays in bunk beds at pilgrims' hostels made me take the bus instead of attempting the walking experience.

"Come to Santiago, that's where the action is" they announced on the radio the days before the 25th of July. I arrived on the day before the Day of Saint James. Across the squares of the town there was a carnival atmosphere with entertainments, theatre and music, and in the streets around the Cathedral the souvenir stalls were lined up in rows selling small figurines of Saint James, crucifixes, pilgrims of plastic and other trinkets.

On the great festive day there were huge crowds in the square in front of the Cathedral, where the mass for Saint James was to be celebrated. The queue for the crypt, where the bodily remains of the Apostle are said to be kept, ended in the street. At the entrance portal, el Pórtico de la Gloria, the tourists were flocking and photographing each other with their hands placed on the plinth on which the famous saint is standing. They touched it with three fingers while smiling to the cameras. According to the tradition, you should express three wishes in your mind while you touch the foot of the Apostle.

In the crowded Cathedral, the pilgrims were standing in line waiting to receive the blessing of the priest. In keeping with tradition, they carried the Pilgrims of Saint James' marks, the walking stick and the small scallop hanging on their rucksack. In their robust walking shoes and other equipment from well-stocked sports shops they were watching the enormous censer, which was swung back and forth in the church and soon filled the room with its distinctive strong aroma. In the evening, there was a spectacular show of fireworks, and the bars were serving wine and beer ad libitum. The national saint was celebrated with a thunderous *fiesta*.

When, the next day, I continued my journey to quieter areas in this green corner of northwestern Spain, I carried along Shirley MacLaine's *The Camino, a Journey of the Spirit*, the easily digestible contents of which were perfect for falling asleep more easily in the evening. In the book the famous Hollywood star initiates the readers into her spiritual pilgrim's walk to Santiago. She divulges how this so-called purification process changed her attitude to life. Among other things, it diminished her interest in material possessions and her constant need to buy new things. However, she didn't complete the whole *camino* on foot and didn't meet the demands of the total purification. Because of a flock of intrusive journalists, who followed at her heels, ultimately she had to take the bus to get some peace.

Even the cult author Paulo Coelho has written about all the trials he was to go through during his walk to Santiago. One of the things he learned was that the road is not for the initiated, but rather for completely ordinary people. However, like Shirley MacLaine, he couldn't either resist the temptation to make his many insights on the way public, contrary to the old mystics' tradition to be quiet and not publically express their knowledge.

The Spanish film director, Luis Buñuel, has a more humorous and less holy version of the *Camino* in his surrealistic film *La Voie Lactée* (The Milky Way). Through the protagonists, two French men, who set out on a walk from Paris to Santiago de Compostela he satirizes Catholicism and heresy.

I saw Santiago de Compostela again some years later in the pouring rain and without the flocks of tourists and pilgrims. The wet streets, the obscure illumination and the big square in front of the Cathedral were reminiscent of an evocative story about a girl, Antonia from Santiago, who was possessed by the Devil. It is one of the author Ramón del Valle Inclán's many strange stories from Galicia and its customs and traditions including, among other things exorcism, which is still practised in the countryside.

A friend of mine, a journalist in La Coruña, had invited me to a conference about *El Camino* to tell about my newly published textbook about the Pilgrim's Road to Santiago. After my presentation, a female Swedish journalist came up to me and insisted that I couldn't publish a book about the Pilgrim's Road without having walked it myself. Totally taken by surprise by her reproach, I began to defend myself with my thorough research of the cultural history of the Camino.

- But you don't know anything about the experiences we, who've walked it, had! You don't even know what it means to throw yourself into all the unforeseen circumstances that you can encounter during the walk! She insisted.

- No, but I suppose you can meet the unforeseen in other ways, too, I replied.

- The pupils have to know what it means to do the walking!

After all the reproaches for my neglect, I suddenly felt like an odd fish among these eager walkers. I asked myself what makes so many people go on this long walk in our times, when airline flights have become one of the most affordable ways to travel! And why Santiago? Do people in our era have a need for more challenging journeys, now that it is as easy as anything to get to the world's end? Or are there also religious motives behind the walk?

After the conference, I got into conversation with one of the participants, Javier, at a bar. We talked about travelling in general.

- Why travel today, when the voyage has become a commercial item? He asked and began to compare the tourists of our time with the explorers of the 13th to 15th centuries.

- At that time, it was the curiosity and the thirst for knowledge that was the motivating force, but today travels implies status, something people just take for granted, he concluded.

- I guess many people are searching for an exciting life through their travels. I suppose there is also a love of adventure in modern man.

- Maybe, but most of them return just as dull as they were before their travels.

- Have you read some of Jung's books?

- Some.

- In "Psychology and Alchemy" he writes that if you really want to develop, you should choose the direct opposite way to that of the usual. For the globetrotter, who gets nervous twitches at the very idea of staying at home on his holiday, the challenge is precisely not to travel, but instead try to find out, why he always wants to be on the move. And for he who never dares to go anywhere, throwing himself out in the unknown and making a long journey could be a means to confront the fear of the unknown and get to learn more about himself.

- That is a very good point, Javier concluded.

- What is then your opinion about the Camino?

- It has just become a new goal for the noisy mass tourism, Javier said and took a gulp of his beer.

WHO WAS MIRANDA?

I was just going to get into a taxi at the airport of Santo Domingo, but I changed my mind at the last moment. There was something about the driver's look and his smile that I didn't like. The appearance was dark and the smile seemed false. With the many scary stories in mind about tourists who got into trouble with a fake taxi, I turned around quickly and went back to the flock that was waiting to get picked up at the entrance. Tall palm trees were swaying outside the airport and the air was warm and humid. I looked around. My blouse was sticking to my back in the afternoon heat, while I was thinking of what to do. I was just about to go to the information desk to ask for help, when I caught sight of a woman with long blond hair and a very pale, almost transparent, skin. I guessed that she was an American.

- Would you have anything against sharing a taxi with me to the city? I asked, and explained my problem.

- Of course not! She said with the openness that is so characteristic of Americans.

- I will be picked up in a moment... You are very welcome to come with me, she added.

Her name was Miranda and she was from Dallas, Texas and was going to have a cancer treatment based on natural medicine at a centre for alternative treatment in Santo Domingo.

When the driver from the alternative cancer centre came, Miranda asked if I could join them in the car. He looked sceptically at me, but when he heard that I spoke Spanish and had come to the Dominican Republic to write a textbook about the country, his face lit up.

- Where are you going to stay? He asked, and I told him the name of the hotel.

- That's not a good hotel. You can stay at Miranda's hotel. I will arrange for you to have a room for half price, but on one condition: you pretend to be a cancer patient for the staff.

- Okay, but what about the hotel, where I have a reservation?

- We will cancel it, he said and threw our suitcases into the luggage room.

I was registered as a cancer patient at a luxury hotel surrounded by palm trees, and at the entrance a guard dressed in a white uniform was receiving the guests. Miranda's room and my own were adjacent with a view to the blue-green Caribbean Sea.

- How was your treatment today? A woman at the reception asked me. I looked at her confusedly, because I had just been doing an interview in the slums and had forgotten all about being a cancer patient. Suddenly it struck me what she meant, and I quickly answered "Fine, thank you" and went up to my room. Generally, I don't like to talk about illnesses, and even if I wasn't ill, the receptionist's compassionate voice was enough to give me the feeling of being a victim.

During the daytime Miranda was at the cancer centre, while I was conducting interviews in Santo Domingo's slums. I tried to avoid the other patients from the cancer centre. I couldn't risk them discovering my deception.

One Saturday we took a day off and went together to a handicraft market in the centre. It was swarming with stalls that displayed basket works, Naïve paintings and other arts and crafts. Miranda bought a small wooden figure of Christ on the Cross, and while we were walking around there, she was talking about the suffering of Christ during the Crucifixion and pressed the figure against her chest.

- It is unbearable for me to think about, she said and with tears emerging from her eyes.

- Let's go and see the Naïve paintings, I said and tried to distract her attention from all the suffering.

- Wow, I just love the colours! She exclaimed when she saw the paintings. She seemed to cheer up at the sight of the lively motifs with dancing people, flowers and trees in bright colours.

- Why do you think that the Dominican painters use so many colours? She asked.

- Maybe it's because of the light and the colours of the nature that inspire them, or perhaps something that comes from within. People here are much less stiff than us in their movements. Have you seen them dance the merengue? And look at that woman and her swaying walk!

- Do you think it is there cheerfulness that makes them choose the bright colours? Miranda asked.

- I don't know; there is also a lot of poverty here.

On the way back, we walked barefoot on the beach with the white sand. I asked her how her cancer treatment was going, but she answered evasively that they couldn't yet give any results, and I didn't refer to the matter any further.

- My brother is paying for it all. He insisted that I should go here, she said.

She had never told me what type of cancer she had and, as we talked about the cancer centre, she tried to distract my attention from her illness and began to talk about the people she had met there. While we were walking in the soft sand, our conversation became more personal, and we told each other about our families.

- My parents always treat me like an invalid. I was anaemic as a child, and apparently, they have got the idea that I am ill... Hey, look at the dark clouds! She exclaimed, and pointed at the sky, which was getting very overcast.

We turned back, but we didn't reach the hotel before the rain came. At first it was only a few drops, but some minutes later, the rain gushed down with such a force that we just remained standing to be soaked. For a moment, Miranda looked as if she had been cleansed of all her burdens. Actually, she was enjoying it, and suddenly we began to laugh while the water fell down on us in a deluge.

When we reached the hotel, we were soaked and the liveried guard couldn't recognise us and wouldn't let us in. "But we are guests at the hotel!" we shouted and then he hurried out to get us some towels and kept bowing and apologising. We dried ourselves and then hurried up to our rooms to change clothes.

The work with my textbook about the Dominican Republic was boring me more and more, and Miranda sensed it.

- Does that book only have to be about social conditions? She asked.

- Almost all the Danish textbooks for the teaching of Spanish are about social conditions in Spain and Latin America.

- You could include some stories about the dictator Trujillo, whom you told me about. That was both interesting and shocking as well, she said.

We took a taxi to Casa de Caoba, one of Trujillo's abandoned houses, which was outside Santo Domingo. The driver drove along the seaside and showed us the place where the dictator was murdered in 1961.

Two boys in ragged clothes came towards us, and we asked them to show us the dictator's house. There was mould on the walls and the paint was peeling off. I imagined the bedroom where the dictator had molested several under-age girls. When Trujillo saw a beautiful girl, he sent for her. Whether or not she was underage did not matter to him. The terrified parents could not do anything, if the dictator had an eye on their daughter.

- How terrible! Was he a Catholic? Miranda exclaimed.

Her religiosity irritated me, but it was never boring to discuss with her. It forced me to sharpen my own arguments, and she always listened attentively to my opinions.

After Miranda's remark on my textbook, I gradually lost interest in working on it. At night, I lay sleeplessly pondering about it. Even her suggestion about Trujillo didn't help. The whole project seemed absurd to me. But what was I going to do with the travelling scholarship I had been awarded to write the book? I decided to go to Haiti for a few days to get away from everything.

When I returned to Santo Domingo, I went to visit Miranda at the hotel. She flung her arms around my neck and insisted that I should stay at her room the last few nights before I went home. To the staff of the hotel I just said that I was cured of my cancer.

We celebrated New Year's Eve together and had dinner in the restaurant, which was in a rock cave, where you could hear the water trickle down the rock wall. We wore our finest dresses and in honour of the occasion, Miranda drank champagne. That night she also, quite unexpectedly, began to talk about her parents.

- They make me depressed. Each time I visit them, they always worry about my health. They never worry about my brother. I can't stand them.

- But it's your right to live as you want to.

She was quiet for a moment and looked down,

- It's easier said than done. I am economically dependent on them.

- But can't you find a job, so that you can break free from them?

- Right now, I don't have the strength to work.

She didn't look very ill apart from her pale skin, but it was not an unhealthy pallor.

- Have you talked to a psychologist about your problems?

- No, no way! She exclaimed and I chose not to refer to the subject anymore.

- Shall we pay and take a taxi back to the hotel? There is only one hour left to midnight.

When we returned to the hotel, there was a New Year's ball in the salon. We sat down at a table near the dance floor. Children, the young and the old alike were moving their hips in time with the merengue music. One of the guests asked if we wanted to dance, and soon we also formed part of the swaying company.

- My parents would die if they saw me now! Miranda raised her arms in the air, and with slightly stiff movements, she began to move her hips.

- Miranda, let's not talk about your parents now, let's have fun!

We were swirled in the monotone rhythm of the merengue dance that went on and on, and Miranda's cheeks became more and more red. Her eyes were sparkling. It struck twelve, and we hugged each other. People began to throw streamers, we were served champagne, and outside the sky was filled with fireworks. When we returned to the hotel room, Miranda showed me photos of her brother and his family, and I showed her my daughters and my husband.

On my last day in Santo Domingo, we decided to see the famous Columbus monument, an enormous bombastic mausoleum, where Columbus's bodily remains are said to be stored. The monument also functions as a lighthouse. Its beams can even be seen in the neighbouring island of Puerto Rico.

In the evening, when we were sitting in our beds talking, I asked for Miranda's phone number and address. She looked at me with her pale blue eyes that seemed sad.

- I am not sure that we will see each other again, she said.

- Why? I am sure that we will meet again, I insisted, and she wrote her address and phone number down in my notebook. I said that I would come and visit her, but she just sent me an inscrutable smile and thanked me for the wonderful days we had together. She would never forget them.

In the morning, when I woke up and was to leave for the airport, she had already gone to the cancer centre. It surprised me that she didn't even leave a message with a farewell greeting.

After my return to Denmark, I decided to drop the textbook project and instead created an exhibition about the Dominican Republic at a local library. While I was preparing the exhibition, and sorting my photos from the trip, I thought about Miranda. I missed the discussions with her and the mutual respect we had for our differences.

One evening I tried to call her, but a voice informed me that the number did not exist. I contacted some friends in the US and asked them to find some information about her, but after one week's research they wrote to me that neither did her address.

I never heard from her again, but I will always remember our friendship that so disturbingly broke into my book project.

THE BLACK AND WHITE ISLAND

There was a silence at the table when I asked the Family Martínez about the popular Dominican dance *merengue* and its African roots.

- The indigenous population in the Dominican Republic were the Taino Indians, the father said breaking the embarrassing silence.

- But the skin colour of the population must be evidence that they are descendants of Africans, I objected and shortly after realised that this was something that I shouldn't talk any more about.

- The dark-skinned are Haitian seasonal workers, the father added with an emphasis on Haitian.

The eldest son of the family had been an exchange student in Denmark and lived with a family who knew one of my friends. I met the son and he told me to make contact with his family. I had corresponded with the family's eldest daughter, who promised me that they would take good care of me while I was in Santo Domingo.

The family lived in a large house in a wealthy neighbourhood. The furnishings were in a truly American style, with pastel-coloured bedrooms and in the bathroom everything was light pink, the towels, the bath tub, the washbasin and the toilet. Even the food they served was American.

- What does your family say when you are travelling so far all alone? The mother asked me after yet another silence.

- They think it's exciting.

- Do they really? ... But you must miss your husband and your daughters, she said with a sceptical tone of voice.

- Yes, of course I do, but this trip is part of my work. I have come here to write a textbook about the Dominican Republic.

The eldest daughter drove me to the hotel.

- Did I say something wrong during the dinner? I asked her.

- Our African heritage is a subject that we Dominicans don't talk about. Me and my mother and my sisters all straighten our hair to hide all the traces of our Negroid origin.

- Oh, I didn't know at all that you are mulattos. You can't see it at all.

- No, and we do everything to hide it.

- But what about your father? He looks European.

- Yes, he is of Spanish origin. His parents emigrated from Spain.

The next day I went to a bookstore in Santo Domingo to buy some books about Dominican culture and history. The shop assistant came with some books that he strongly recommended me to read and whispered that the Dominicans were a bunch of racists. He showed his ID card to me.

- The big "I" on the card means "Indio", Indian, but I am a mulatto. The Dominicans claim to be descended from the Taino Indians and are divided into dark and light Indians. I belong to the "Indios oscuros", dark Indians. It is not good form in this country to talk about the African heritage. It's because of our history, he explained and went out to find some more books upon the subject.

It was not until later, when I decided to visit Haiti, that I began to understand what it was all about. The warnings resonated with me when I began to inquire about trips to Haiti, and at the hotel it was not possible to get any information about that. They just recommended me to go to Punta Cana or some other Dominican beach resort. Why did I want to go to Haiti of all places, a country that was totally ruled by voodoo? At length, I found a small travel agency that arranged weekend tours to Port-au-Prince with a stopover at a hotel and the opportunity to be picked up at the bus station and brought to the hotel.

On the bus to Port-au-Prince I sat beside an ophthalmologist, who went to Haiti every month to treat eye diseases. When he heard that I was from Denmark, he brightened up.

- Is Denmark a republic?

I explained him the political system and told him about our queen, whom you could meet shopping in the streets of Copenhagen.

- Isn't she risking being shot?

- I wouldn't consider it likely, and she doesn't have any real power.

The bus made a short break at a little bar, and as soon as the passengers got out, a flock of young boys in ragged clothes began to pull at my handbag and asked for money. The ophthalmologist pushed them away as if they were a pack of dogs and threatened them with his fist.

- They are Haitian immigrants. That's why they are so infuriating. A pack of scoundrels, that's what they are!

He invited me for a coke in the café.

- Why do you want to visit Haiti of all places? It is primitive and underdeveloped, and it is also a dangerous country. I always sleep with a gun under my pillow when I am there. They can do anything after their stupid voodoo rituals, he said and poured more coke into my glass.

- Isn't it a very poor country?

- It's their own fault, because they don't want to work. They just want to practise their voodoo. Everything is influenced by the voodoo in that country.

Coming to Haiti was like coming to Africa. The people's colour of the skin was darker and the women wore gaily coloured dresses with African patterns and big turbans on their heads, and some of them were carrying their babies on their backs.

The bus stopped at a small station with a bench outside. I looked anxiously around for the man who was to take me to my hotel.

- Weren't you going to be picked up by some-body? The ophthalmologist asked me before leaving.

- Yes, they will come soon, I answered.

The small bus station was soon empty, and I took a seat on the bench, while I, slightly panic-stricken, was thinking about what to do if no-body appeared. If I was kidnapped, would my family ever get to know what happened to me? I was thinking about my daughters and my husband and about Miranda with whom I had become so associated.

A young guy, who looked like one of the young men in Pasolini's film "The Thousand and One Nights", came to me and asked in a French that was very difficult to understand, if he could help. "Non, non, merçi", I said shortly with all the warnings in mind.

I was on the verge of tears, when a middle-aged man with a tired expression turned up.

- David Walter, he said, and offered me his hand.

- I was afraid that you wouldn't come.

- I didn't know that the bus had already arrived, he said and asked me to go with him to his car.

We drove through a slum-like area, where the children were playing in black puddles. Not far from all the misery was the ex-dictator Baby Doc's chalk-white Palais Nacional, which sat in state like an enormous Victoria sponge over the miserable surroundings – the same palace that collapsed during the big earthquake that hit Haiti so hard in 2010.

- Do you want to take a picture?

- I would prefer one of the kids playing in the puddle.

He didn't answer.

The higher we got up the slope, the wealthier the surroundings were, and the more stylish were the villas, which were in sharp contrast to the shabby life down in the valley. Outside one of the villas, which was on the way to the hotel, there was an interminable queue with poor Haitians.

- Why are they standing there?

- It's the Dominican Republic's consulate. They all want to apply for residence permit to work in the country.

- And in the Dominican Republic they want to go to New York, where they are discriminated and are living a miserable life as illegal immigrants.

- Yes, that's the pecking order we have on this island.

The hotel was high up in the neighbourhood Pétionville with a view to the sea. It was surrounded by a wall, both at the gate and at the entrance to the lobby there were heavily armed guards.

- Would you like to see a voodoo ceremony tonight? You can participate with a French group, Mr Walter asked.

- Thank you, but I am a little tired.

Actually, I just looked forward to sitting in my room after dinner and enjoying the Naïve paintings on the walls and the view of the sea and to read a book about Haiti that I had bought.

- Most tourists are just wild about seeing a voodoo ceremony.

- I would prefer to see Port au Prince tomorrow.

- As you wish. I will see to it that Emmanuel will pick you up tomorrow at ten o'clock.

The next morning, I waited over half an hour in the lobby and was about give up the city-tour, when a good-looking guy turned up and asked if I was the one who wanted to see Port-au-Prince. He had a dancing walk and when we were in the car, he played some rhythmic music and joined in with all the songs while driving. On the way to the centre we stopped at a market hall, where he wanted to buy some fruit for his mother. I took a picture of a heavy woman with a wash-bowl filled with bananas on her head. She became furious, threatened me with her fist and shouted all kinds of things at me with a shrill voice and everybody turned around. I turned off my camera at once and put it in my bag, but the woman involved everybody who was near her. Her piercing voice could be heard far out in the street, and I feared that they would all throw themselves on me. I looked at Emmanuel, but he just rocked on with his dancing walk and a discreet smile.

The centre was a complete chaos. Overfilled buses painted in vivid colours and figures, trucks with barrel stands propped with people and pedestrians, who were running between the cars and the buses. Everybody wanted to get on, but nothing seemed to function.

A sharp pain suddenly shot through my stomach, and at last I had to ask Emmanuel if we could stop at a pharmacy.

- What's wrong?

- I have a pain in my stomach.

- We will drive to my father, he is a voodoo priest and he heals illnesses.

I imagined some sort of witch doctor who was going to sacrifice a bird and other ferocious rituals, but with the great pain I was ready to accept anything. Emmanuel beeped through the chaotic traffic and shouted from the car window to those who were in front of us to let us pass because he had a sick passenger.

We stopped at a low green house with a large garden in the outskirts of the city where some children were playing. They all came running to the car when Emmanuel got out. He whispered something to them, and they ran away. We entered the house, where a tiny man with friendly eyes welcomed us.

- This is my father.

Emmanuel said something to him in Creole. We went into a room filled with streamers in different colours hanging from the loft and at the end there was a voodoo altar with bottles, plates with food and some cardboard masks. The father asked me to come to the altar and then he put his hand on my stomach and chanted a long series of unintelligible words. Then he took a bottle with a red fluid and moved it in circular movements over my stomach and said something to Emmanuel.

- My father asks if you have a husband? I nodded.

- He says that your pains have something to do with him, and if I could solve the problem with him, the pains would diminish.

Perhaps it was my fear of infidelity, I thought.

The father now made a healing herbal tea for me. He handed me the cup with a dark green fluid, and Emmanuel explained that I should drink it all in small sips and send positive thoughts to my husband. While I drank the bitter tea, I thought with each sip of my husband and all the positive things we had together and all the backing I got for my need to travel alone. The pain vanished gradually. Emmanuel said something in Creole to his father and he nodded to me with a smile.

- Are you ready to go now? Emmanuel said and we continued our drive to the tones of Caribbean rhythms and Emmanuel's squalling song.

He stopped the car at a shopping centre.

- You can't go home without having seen the Haitian art. We are very proud of it, he said.

Inside the centre there were several art galleries with Naïve paintings in bright colours with surrealistic motives. One of the gallery owners told me that André Breton, the Father of Surrealism, had visited Haiti and was totally spellbound by the art.

I bought a miniature, which represented a dreamlike landscape with flowers as big as trees in blue-green shades.

- If I had more money and more room in my suitcase, I would buy some more of them. Only these paintings could bring me back to Haiti.

- All our art is influenced by voodoo. That's the secret behind it, Emmanuel said.

When I returned to Santo Domingo, Mrs. Martinez called and asked anxiously where I had been, because they would have invited me on a weekend tour to a wonderful bathing place with golf courses and all the heart could desire.

- I have been in Port-au-Prince in the week-end.

She was silent for some seconds and I heard her sigh.

- I wish you a nice trip back to Denmark.

Following this talk, I never heard from the Family Martinez again.

MACABRE TANGO

During my student years at the University of Copenhagen, I got to know Tomás and visited him now and then in his room. Tomás was from Córdoba in Argentina and had come to Denmark as a refugee during the last dictatorship. Once, while talking, we heard a drill from the adjacent apartment. Tomás turned pale and he became silent as the grave. I asked him what the matter was. "Nothing", he answered in a grim tone of voice, and I ended up leaving, because I couldn't get a single word out of him.

Tomás was very politically active, but I didn't like him when he was talking about politics. He became so dogmatic and self-important, some-times even aggressive, and as far as possible, I tried to avoid the subject, as it would certainty lead to quarrels. He also criticized me for not being sufficiently politically active. But Tomás was also homesick, and I enjoyed his company when we had *mate,* and he told me about Argen-tina and its culture and customs. Then he was himself and showed his sensitivity and awoke

119

my desire to see his native country, which I came to visit several times.

Many years later, on one of my visits to Buenos Aires, I went for a drive with my friends Tamara and Enrique. We drove through a dreary neighbourhood with run-down buildings. Suddenly Enrique reduced the speed and stopped under a highway. He wanted to show me something. At first sight it looked like some excavation behind a pane of glass. On the sand, there were a lot of small flags with names on them. These were the names of the persons who had disappeared during Argentina's dictatorship, Enrique explained. Club Atlético was not actually an athletics club, but rather a cover name for one of the dictatorship's many secret interrogation centres. It got its name from the nearby football-club, Boca Juniors. Suddenly, everything I had read about the 30.000 who disappeared became more vivid to me.

I asked Tamara and Enrique if they knew anyone, who had disappeared during the dictatorship. They nodded with a distant look in their eyes, but they showed a reluctance to talk about it. "If you want to know more, you can take a guided tour at the ESMA, the Army's Mechanical School, which was one of the biggest interro-

gation centres in Buenos Aires during the dictatorship", they suggested.

I took a taxi to ESMA, which was on the outskirts of the centre. The entire area was surrounded by iron bars. At the entrance, the guard
showed me to a small group of tourists, who
were waiting for a guide.

- Have a seat, the guide will be here soon.

It took a long time, and people began to look
despairingly. A German woman went out to talk
to the guard.

- We have waited for almost an hour!

- She will be here soon, the guard said, completely unaffected by the woman's agitated
voice.

When the girl finally turned up, the German
woman gave her a reprimand, but apparently, it
didn't faze her. *"Traffic problems"*, she said non-
chalantly with her pronounced Spanish accent.

- My name is Inés, just follow me.

We went for a walk in the area and stopped in
front of a white building with dark windows,
which was the most important of the various
interrogation centres. She explained what those
arrested had to go through after having been
brought blindfold to ESMA.

- We have some reconstructed accounts by survivors, who were able to calculate where they were by listening to sounds from trains and the like, she explained.

In an excited tone of voice, she also told us about the 500 children, who were born in different interrogation centres to mothers, who, after giving birth, were executed. The babies were given to the military's friends or relatives, and many of them have had the illusion of being adopted, or even legitimate children.

- Today these children have organized themselves into an association called "Hijos" (Children), and many of them have denounced their parents to the police.

- But how can you trace these children? One of the participants asked.

- The Mothers of Plaza de Mayo do a great job of finding them, and they also help these children to get away from their adoptive parents.

I remembered an Argentine film about the subject and asked her if it didn't cause significant distress if they suddenly had to renounce or leave the parents, who had brought them up?

- In spite of everything they must have been fond of them as parents.

Maybe I felt provoked by her attitude. I had the feeling that for her there was only one truth that couldn't be questioned.

Her eyes revealed that she considered my question improper. In a raised voice she underlined that it was the children's right to know where they came from, and that they, when they found out the background for their adoption, would cease to be fond of their parents. While she was talking, I got the suspicion that she was one of these children. Both her age and the insistent way in which she spoke about them, suggested it. This might explain why she had chosen to be a guide at this place. She might also have been influenced by the generally increasing tendency among young people to break with their parents.

The tour ended in the main building, where there were a couple of showrooms and a café. The walls were decorated with drawings of torture victims and their tormentors, who were applying different torture methods. While I was looking at them, I remembered Tomás and the sound of the drill, which made him lose his composure.

I went out to get a taxi.

Did you go on a tour at ESMA? The driver asked and looked at me with an unpleasant expression.

- Yes, I wanted to know some more about the dictatorship.

- Where are you from?

- From Denmark.

- *Dinamarca...* Don't you have a famous football player in Denmark?

But before I had answered, he again began to talk about ESMA.

- They give the tourists a very one-sided presentation of the dictatorship. They never tell about the Montoneros' bloody assassinations... Maybe you don't know so much about the history of Argentina... Montoneros was a leftist urban guerilla movement... Their assassinations provoked the military coup in 1976. They were Peronists like Cristina, our president, and that's why you don't hear anything negative about them...

I met his eyes in the mirror and got an unpleasant feeling.

- I want to get out here, I said.

- Didn't you say that you wanted to go to the centre? He insisted.

- I want to get out here.

- As you wish, he said and applied the brake sharply. I paid and hurried out. A few minutes later I found another taxi.

Tamara and Enrique called me and asked if I liked the guided tour at ESMA. They knew an artist who would like to take me out and tell me some more about "the Dirty War", as the dictatorship was also called. He had lived in Buenos Aires during all the seven years it lasted.

Alberto picked me up at the hotel and wanted to show me La Boca. We went for a walk in the old immigrant neighbourhood, where the tango was born. While we walked around in the humble streets in the misty afternoon sun, he told me about the crowds of immigrants that arrived at the turn of the century from Italy and Spain, and about the dreadful conditions the lived under upon arrival. But he didn't say a word about the "Dirty War".

- Now I want to invite you for a pizza as the Italians did it when they arrived in Argentina, Alberto said.

We took a seat in a small restaurant, which was decorated like an Italian pizzeria in the beginning of the 20th century with the counter and the walls covered in dark wood. Alberto ordered a *pizza faina*, a pizza covered with a chickpea-dough.

While we were eating, he began to tell me about the origins of the tango. Finally, I screwed up my courage and asked him how he had experienced the dictatorship.

- Why do you want to talk about that depressing era? There are so many other and more interesting things in Buenos Aires.

I didn't know what to answer, but he anticipated me.

- You always had to be careful of what you said. You could never know what might go on. There were informers everywhere. If, for some reason, you ended up on the secret list of the police, it could mean death even if you hadn't been involved in any political activity. To have acquaintances could be fatal.

- Did you also dance the tango during the dictatorship?

- Many of the *milongas* were closed, because the regime didn't like big gatherings. Even some tango songs were censored.

When I began to ask him about the disappeared, he tried to evade the question and directed the conversation to his upcoming art exhibition, which he talked about for the rest of the afternoon.

126

The next day I went to the impressive bookstore *el Ateneo* – a former cinema whose interior reminded me of the Royal Theatre in Copenhagen to find books about the dictatorship.

The shop assistant recommended me the novel *Hay unos tipos abajo* (There are some types down there) by Antonio Dal Masetto. The book gave me a vivid picture of the atmosphere in those traumatic years. The main character, the journalist Pablo, is informed by his girlfriend about two men sitting in a car outside the entrance to the building where he lived. When the same car also appears the following day, he suspects them to be spying on him, even though he had never been politically active. The novel, through Pablo, describes how people were struck by panic, because nobody could feel secure.

During my continued searching on the Internet, I got into contact with Maria, who was working for an organization that collected accounts from witnesses by survivors of torture, and she offered me a guided tour of an interrogation centre.

I met Maria and her friend Ernesto in the neighbourhood Floresta, and they took me to

Automotores Orletti, a car repair shop, which was bought by the regime and used secretly as an interrogation centre, where about 300 people were interrogated under torture.

Ernesto unlocked the metal gate and we entered a dark and ice-cold hall.

- Here the arrested, who were blindfold, were brought and had to wait until it was their turn.

With a shiver I caught sight of some names that were scratched on the wall. They probably knew their destiny. We went upstairs where the former interrogation-rooms were. After the torture sessions, most of the arrested disappeared without trace. Many were thrown into the sea from aeroplanes, Ernesto explained.

The only encouraging part of this tour was Ernesto's story about a young couple, which, in spite of their mistreated condition, was able to plan their escape. They found out that the executioners used to get drunk at night and saw a possibility to escape after they had passed out. One night they succeeded in stealing the executioners' keys, while they were sleeping, and they got out of the building. They crossed the railway track just outside the centre and ran away. Immediately after, a train came and blocked the path of their former persecutors. Miraculously, they escaped all the way to Mexico.

Ernesto closed the metal gate and had to go back to his work. I was freezing and asked Maria if she would have coffee with me in a café. When I asked her about her own experience with the military dictatorship, she put a finger before her mouth and whispered: "Shhh, you never know if somebody is listening."

The same afternoon I needed to rid my mind of all the unpleasant insights at a distance and decided to visit Confitería Ideal, originally a tea salon from 1912, which had become one of the most famous dancing places in Buenos Aires. However, hardly had I got my tango shoes on, before an elderly man in a striped black suit asked me to dance. I told him that I was a *principiante*, a beginner, but that didn't matter at all, he assured me with a smile. We sailed down the dancing floor under the huge chandelier, and now I understood what it meant to be led by an experienced tango dancer. During the short break between the two rounds, however, I discovered something in his eyes that I disliked. It was as if his eyes suddenly became dark and tough. The tones of the next tango flowed out into the room and once again we glided on the floor in time with the music, and while he was leading me, I thought, with a slight shiver, that

this man could very well be one of the executioners from the dictatorship who were still at
large.

ABOUT MYTHS AND TRAINS

On this trip to Buenos Aires, almost everything took me by surprise. It was as if the Argentine capital began to show me its seamy sides – sides that you might not always discover at the first visit, when you walk around with Rose-coloured glasses, which through time have been created by people's need to glorify certain places and their history.

I landed at Ezeiza airport on a cold day in July, in the middle of the Argentine winter. At my hotel the interior was decorated in line with the Argentine tango in the 30s with pictures of famous tango singers on the walls. My room was furnished in the same style: old furniture with twisted lines and white lace curtains. In the bathroom there were chrome-plated taps, a mirror with a golden frame, thick pink towels and a piece of scented soap at the edge of the bathtub. However, the functioning of the electric and electronic equipment was as miserable as the décor was thoroughly feminine. The Internet only functioned sporadically, and in the evening, when I wanted to send an email to my husband about the day's experiences, the connection was interrupted. When I, on the first evening, wanted to take a warm bath, there was a power cut, and the beautiful room was in total darkness for half an hour. During my stay in Buenos Aires, I experienced power cuts almost daily. Most inopportune was the one that came when I was walking up the stairs (I didn't dare take the elevator for fear of getting stuck in it for hours). I couldn't see anything, but I could hear somebody standing near me. The situation recalled a Swedish horror film I had seen long ago. I could hear the person breathing in the dark and didn't dare take another step. I sighed of relief when I heard other guests coming out of their rooms, and unknown voices began to talk in the dark on the staircase. Suddenly, the lights were turned on again and everybody smiled at each other in relief.

Breakfast was served in the hotel's little café, which was furnished like a dancing place for tango with pictures of the legendary tango singer Carlos Gardel in a golden frame. Each morning the coffee and the croissants could be enjoyed to the sound of his slightly feminine voice. But why did Gardel always take precedence over so many other fabulous tango singers? One of the reasons for creating the myth is said to be his close relationship to his mother. A large proportion of the immigrants in Argentina are Italian, and Italian men are said to adore their mammas. Gardel's mother was an immigrant from Toulouse in France and she made a living by ironing. Both her immigrant background, her origin from humble conditions and Gardel's idolization of his mother are said to have contributed to the creation of the myth. Gardel's fame and his impeccable well-groomed appearance were a proof of the possibility to climb up the social ladder. But his sudden death in a plane crash in 1935 is said to have contributed most to his fame. Death often plays an important part in the creation of the myth. Not only in Argentina, but all over Latin America people were crying over the loss of the eternally smiling singer. And there are a great number of celebrities, who have become immortal after their deaths, among others the Colombian drug lord Pablo Escobar, to whom the poor pay homage to as a saint.

The hotel and its adulation of Gardel, was also a confirmation of the subject that I had come to speak about at a congress for Hispanic literature and culture in Buenos Aires. The inauguration took place at the Faculty of Law in an enormous, monumental building with big pillars at the entrance. The many speeches in the assembly hall corresponded to the building, of which the bombastic façade was a stark contrast to the run-down interior. Some of the participants fell asleep during the speeches and opened their eyes bewilderedly during the subsequent applause. Afterwards, we were invited for a drink and some snacks. A young Norwegian woman said hello to me and told me that we were the only Scandinavians at the congress and that we would give our papers in the same premises. This was her first visit to Buenos Aires, and when she heard that I had visited the city several times before, she asked me to recommend some places where you could learn tango.

The papers were given in different buildings in the neighbourhood of Recoleta, not very far from the famous cemetery where Evita Perón and other celebrities are buried in expansive mausoleums. The building where we were to give our papers looked from outside like a gothic church. The interior was rather run-down. The premises were damaged and poorly maintained, the paint on the walls was peeling off, and the furniture was old and worn, but the worst was the lack of heating in the middle of the winter with temperatures around 5 degrees Celsius.

The subject of my paper was the Swedish professor Inger Enkvist's book about the Latin

American worship of myths. I had, with great enthusiasm, read some of her books about teaching and education. Enkvist is a woman who is not afraid of stating her honest opinion, and for many years she has been outside the prevalent discourse with her criticism of the Swedish educational reforms of the 60s and the 70s, which, according to her, have caused a decrease in the knowledge level of the pupils. With the same enthusiasm, I read her criticism of the Latin American icons, among others Evita Perón, Frida Kahlo, Che Guevara and Maradona. In her book, Enkvist points out the paradox that most of these personages don't deserve the halo the masses have given them.

The lecturers were each introduced by the moderator, an Argentinian woman. We had twenty minutes for each paper, a time limit that is seldom kept by Latin Americans, who often have quite a different attitude to time than we Europeans. In return, I was brought up to always respect the rules of time. For the same reason, I had read my paper aloud a few times before presenting it. Nor, for that matter, did I want to make the same error of reading too fast, as many of the Latin Americans did. When I had read about half of my paper, the moderator's harsh voice interrupted me:

- You have four minutes left! You can make a summary of the rest.

I looked uncomprehendingly at her unyeld-ing face and realized that I had to accept, even if I was sure that she was mistaken. The rest was summarized. Afterwards, there was an unpleas-ant atmosphere in the room. A member of the audience asked me if the positions to which I had referred were also my own.

- Not all of them, but some, and now I con-cluded that the contents of my paper were not well received.

Later, we were served coffee and cookies in the ice-cold vestibule. My Norwegian colleague came up to me and asked how you can condemn people like Frida Kahlo and Carlos Gardel. "Fri-da Kahlo was a victim!" My attempt to explain that Enkvist's point was not to condemn them, but rather to discuss that tendency to promote individuals to myths, was pointless. Inadvertent-ly, I happened to touch on a sore point.

An Italian woman, who was a tourist guide in Patagonia, told me that on one of her tours an American guy had begun to discuss *the Falkland Islands* with an Argentinian guy. The mere use of the name *Falkland Islands* was enough to provoke the Argentinian guy, who shouted that their name was *Las Malvinas* and called him a bloody

Briton. He was just about to hit the American, who saved his neck when he revealed his American nationality.

I decided not to participate in the congress the next day. Instead I took the train to Tigre, a small town at the delta of the river Paraná, about 30 kilometres from Buenos Aires. The sun was shining and there were many passengers on the way to this popular destination for excursions. The train started, but it proceeded at a glacial pace and it all seemed extremely old fashioned. At every stop, new street vendors entered. One of them put a pack of Kleenex on the lap of each passenger and gathered them up afterwards hoping that the packages were opened so that they could claim money from them. The next vendour had a ballpoint pen for the passengers and the third exclaimed:

I have five children who are starving. Have mercy with me and my family...

Suddenly the train stopped. After fifteen minutes, people began to become exasperated. The woman next to me shouted:

- It's a lack of respect!

Her face looked tired and run-down. I asked her if this happened often.

- Our transport system is bloody awful! The politicians don't care about us. Look what happened after the railway accident at the Once neighbourhood.

I hadn't heard about it.

- In 2012, there was an accident at the Once station in Buenos Aires. A train crashed into a dead end and fifty people died. But do you think that they want to do something about the trains? No, they don't do a damn thing! Cristina, our president, doesn't care! She hasn't done anything, her hoarse tobacco-voice shouted.

People got heated, accusations were flying through the wagon. A ticket inspector hurried through the train claiming he didn't have time to answer any questions. The atmosphere became even more agitated. After almost an hour, the train suddenly started again and continued at the same funereal pace as before to Tigre.

What a joy it was when I finally sat down in one of the boats that take people around the enormous delta, where all the houses are standing on high stilts because of the regular floods.

The train back to Buenos Aires went with the same snail's pace, but without any unforeseen stops.

- But you should have taken *El tren de la costa* the coast train! On the slow train anything can happen, my friend Tamara exclaimed, terrified, when I told her about my trip.

When I appeared at the congress the next day to hear some papers, I met my Norwegian colleague and her Spanish girlfriend. They greeted me very briefly and hurried away. I could feel a lump in my throat, which reminded me that myths should be treated with great caution.

THE ART OF
IMPROVISATION

The opening of the congress for female Latin American authors in Panama City reminded me in many ways of what I experienced when I asked my way in the city. If I asked people in the street, they were always willing to help. "Go straight ahead and after three blocks, turn right…" The directions, however, seldom led me to my destination, and often, the next person I asked explained that it was in the opposite direction. If I was lucky, it was the right way, but often it required up to several attempts in different directions before I arrived there.

The ceremony was to take place in the auditorium of the university, but when I arrived, the big room was totally empty. I went down to the office, where I spoke to two women, who looked wonderingly and rather uninterestedly at me when I explained that I was invited to the opening of the congress in the auditorium. After a long discussion back and forth they finally decided to help me. They called different offices, and after several telephone calls it turned out that the festivities were to be held in premises other than those originally notified to the participants of the congress.

One of the women called a taxi, for which I had to wait a long time, and when I finally sat in the car, I had no illusions of getting there on time. When I arrived at the right place, which turned out to be one of the main theatres in the city, people were talking outside the entrance. I went to register myself and breathlessly explained to the smiling women that I went to the university auditorium as indicated in their last email. It had been changed, they just said. "Please, have a glass of punch and a snack. The ceremony will not begin until the programme has arrived from the printing office", they explained. Latin Americans are generally socially minded people, and the waiting time was an obvious occasion to get to know each other. Soon the vestibule sounded like a cackling chicken run. When the programme finally arrived, about an hour later than the opening time, it took quite a long time to get all the animatedly talking people into the theatre.

The lack of a sense of observing time and appointments reminded me of my Mexican girlfriend, Cecilia, who made me wait several times in vain with the dinner ready in the oven without ever showing up. When I called her to ask why she didn't come, she just explained, as if it was the most natural thing in the world, that she thought it was following week. Sometimes she didn't even answer the phone. Later, I have figured out that she had the habit of making several appointments at a time and on the appointed day she just chose the party that she found most interesting. At her work, she turns up when it suits her, but she is always forgiven. People usually find it charming, an exotic characteristic, and when they see her dance salsa at the staff parties, everything is forgotten.

The opening ceremony started with an endless series of speeches by the cultural authorities of the city, whose bombastic rhetoric in comparison with the North European tradition for measured speaking and understatement seemed a bit comical. During the speeches, some people went in and out of the hall, while others just continued their chatting – an impoliteness in our part of the world – but, with an eye to the long flows of talk, of which most of them lacked any substance, it was understandable. The ceremony was closed with a show of Panamanian folk dances. Women in vividly coloured wide skirts entered the scene, and when they twirled around during the dance, their skirts resembled enormous fans.

The congress started the next day, and I ticked off the talks I found interesting. When I entered the room where the first paper was to be held, there was nobody there. I ran down to the office, where nobody knew anything, neither about the rooms nor the talks. "How am I going to find the rooms if there are errors in the programme?" I shouted. – "By asking", the woman behind the desk said and continued to chat with her colleagues.

I followed her advice, and, through doing so, I succeeded in attending most of the talks I had marked in the programme. A woman from Buenos Aires apparently considered it her right to interrupt the lecturer as often as she wished. She was an eccentric woman of about 60 with bleached hair that was put up and decorated with a big pink rose. She began to tell the audience about the lecturer's subject, because she apparently thought that she knew more about it.

During the congress several of the participants wondered where I came from. "Dinamarca!" they exclaimed enthusiastically, and it turned out that I was the only North European in the flock. Apparently they didn't know much about Scandinavia. However, some of them knew Hans Christian Andersen. But they found it even more sensational that I travelled alone without my husband. "And what is he doing while you are gone?" one of them exclaimed, and the rest of them immediately woke up. A woman travelling alone in Latin America seemed to be a rare thing. A form of sisterly solidarity with me arose immediately, and I was invited to cafés, shopping trips, sightseeing and many other activities in the afternoon after the lectures.

The Latin American women's care for me was boundless and thwarted my own desire to be alone. They went with me to shoe stores and clothes shops and they consulted the assistants on which dress and size would suit me best. I had chosen a red silk dress, but the women decided that it was too expensive and that we should find another shop, where they had some fabulous dresses at much more reasonable prices. When I finally returned to my hotel room and lay down on my bed with a book, the telephone rang and my companions said that they would come and pick me up in two hours. We were going to a restaurant and afterwards we would visit a fabulous bar, where one of Panama's best singers would sing.

When the congress came to an end, we all went our separate ways. I had a few days left in Panama City and decided to go on a guided tour of the rain forest. I also contacted a language school that offered private lessons at a high level for Spanish teachers. When I asked if they had someone who could teach me about Panamanian culture, politics and language, they immediately recommended Alfredo. A fantastic teacher, they said. Americans just love him, they assured me.

I was sitting in the school's waiting room accompanied by a large chattering parrot in a cage. A middle-aged man with creased khaki-coloured trousers and a chequered shirt came in and introduced himself as Alfredo. My first lesson was about the differences between European and Panamanian Spanish. Alfredo had brought some exercises with the verbal conjugation.

- But I am a teacher of Spanish and I have learned the verbal conjugation!

- I have taught many teachers of Spanish from the US, and they always want something with verbs, he objected with a smile.

- But I have studied Spanish at the university and I have learned the grammar. Couldn't you find some exercises with idiomatic expressions instead?

Alfredo promised to find a list with idiomatic expressions for the last lesson. Now he wanted to tell me a little about Panama and pulled down a map of Central America. With a certain eagerness, he grabbed the pointer and pointed at Panama.

- Panama shares borders with Costa Rica and Colombia, and you can sail through the Panama Canal from the Atlantic Ocean to the Pacific Ocean, he explained with a big smile before recommending me to go for a sail on the Canal.

- I already have…

Alfredo anticipated me and told me far and wide about the big locks in the canal and all the huge cargo ships that sailed through it. I asked if he knew Maersk that had several big cargo ships waiting for permission to sail through the canal.

- Yes, it's a German company.

- No, it's Danish!

- No, it is not! He insisted in a slightly paternalistic tone. He got up, looked at his watch and said that the lesson was finished now. Before I left, he said that it had been very interesting to teach me and that he looked forward to the next lesson, which would be about the Panamanian culture.

The next day Alfredo received me beaming with joy and said that he had a surprise for me. He took out a large picture of a smiling woman in a very wide pleated skirt with laces and red embroideries, exactly like the ones the women wore at the folk dances at the inauguration of the congress.

- It is *la pollera*, Panama's national dress, he explained with a certain solemnity in his voice and began to tell me expansively about the variants of the skirt in the different parts of the country and the many national dances. Suddenly, he got up and stepped out onto the middle of the floor and began to make small dance steps while he was humming a song.

- It's *el tamborito*, he said, while he was swaying back and forth.

When he sat down again, I asked if he could tell me something about the political conditions in the country and about what the Panamanians thought about the transfer of the former dictator Noriega to a prison in Panama. He frowned.

- Noriega is a nasty guy, who has caused a lot of damage to the country, but fortunately he is in prison … it is on the bank of the Canal and can be seen from the boat, if you sail on it … I would certainly recommend you to go on that sailing trip before you go home.

- I have already made it and I have also seen the prison.

He looked at his watch and said that we might as well stop the lesson now because there were only ten minutes left.

The last lesson with Alfredo was about idiomatic expressions. He had brought a number of Panamanian proverbs and suggested that I could read them aloud in Spanish and then we could talk about the ones I didn't understand. I began to read, and Alfredo gave long and lengthy explanations which needed further clarification. I went on reading, but while I was reading, it was suddenly very quiet, and when I looked up, Alfredo had fallen asleep and his head dangled to one side. I stopped the reading and coughed slightly. Alfredo started and looked very confused. With a smile and as if nothing had happened he just said that he had got to bed very late last night. He said that he had been so glad to teach me and that I if I came back to Panama, I should not hesitate to contact him. Before I left, he added that right from the beginning he had felt that the chemistry between us was so good.

I was standing in the air-conditioned lobby of my hotel waiting for my airport-transfer, for which I had paid for n advance. After half an hour I went out into the humid heat to look for the car. There were dark clouds in the sky and the air was heavy with rain. The driver never appeared. A receptionist called the company to ask where the car was, but they didn't know anything about the order. The receptionist ordered a taxi, which drove me to the airport in the pouring rain. I got there at the last minute.

THE DRIVER WITH THE
MYSTERIOUS SMILE

Hotel Palmer House has exits to four different streets, and people swarm in and out of the enormous building, as if it were a department store. The bill was already paid and the money drawn from my card without my approval, when I handed my plastic key to the receptionist: easy and handy if you don't want any closer contact between the staff and the customers. At Palmer House it is the grandiose lobby in a heavily ornamented beaux-arts style which is the attraction of the hotel. When you step into the lobby, you get the impression of something very elegant, of the pomp and circumstance of colonial times. However, my room didn't live up to the façade of the hotel at all. It was dreary and with overlooking a railway track on which the local train passed by every half hour with a rasping sound.

It was not with any melancholy that I went out on the street to wait for my airport transfer. Not until fifteen minutes after the appointed time did a white car appeared with AIRPORT EXPRESS painted on it. The driver jumped out of the car, snatched my suitcase, threw it in with the other suitcases and opened the sliding door without even apologizing for the delay. He drove at a breakneck speed and was in the middle of a quarrel on the phone, apparently with his wife or his girlfriend. He was a Latino, a Colombian, I guessed from his Spanish pronunciation.

Hey, you have the same ring as I have! The woman sitting beside me exclaimed enthusiastically. She put her hand beside mine. Her silver ring with a little pearl surrounded by to small flowers and a couple of leaves was a true replica of mine.

- Where did you buy yours? She asked.

- In Copenhagen. And what about you? I asked.

- At Tiffany's.

I pretended that my ring was also of the expensive sort, even though I didn't pay more than about a hundred dollars for it. After the arrival to the airport all the passengers spread in different directions. *Have a nice trip wherever you are going,* the woman with the ring said just when I was about to ask her if we could exchange emails. I liked the combination of her unsnobbish behavior and her evident inclination for precious things, but she was already gone.

I looked everywhere for the United Airlines-sign to check my luggage, but I couldn't see it anywhere. At the information desk they informed me that United Airlines didn't even fly from Midway Airport.

- You have to go to the O'Hare Airport. I stared at them totally dumbfounded.

- How long does it take to get to O'Hare from here?

- About an hour, the man said without showing any interest at all in my problem.

With a lump in my throat I thought about calling Airport Express to complain, but on their receipt it said - I now discovered– to Midway Airport.

- You can just take a taxi to O'Hare, ma'am, the man at the information desk said.

Without answering I just dashed off and jostled through the queue with an attitude that claimed *"Sorry, but I am late, my plane is leaving..."*

I took the first taxi that came along and asked breathless:

- How long does it take to get to O'Hare airport?

With a peculiar smile and a heavy accent, he answered that it took about an hour and that we would get there on time.

When I stepped into the car my book about Israel fell out of my bag together with a pack of biscuits. The driver handed me the book and the biscuits.

- Where are you from? I asked when he began to drive.

- I am a Palestinian, he said briefly.

- I am from Denmark, I said, but it didn't seem to interest him at all.

- How long have you lived in the US?

- Eleven years.

- And what about your family? Are they also here?

- No, they live in Ramallah, he answered and took a gulp of his coffee with a long slurping sound.

- How much time is there left? I asked after a quarter of an hour's drive.

- About half an hour. You will get there on time, he said with another enigmatic smile.

I looked out of the window but couldn't see any road signs to the O'Hare airport, and the area seemed almost completely deserted. Could this be a fake taxi? At Buenos Aires' airport they distributed small notes warning the newly arrived tourists of fake taxis and recommended them to order a taxi from the airport office. But his smile wasn't necessarily malicious. Smiles can also be used as a defence. Even chimpanzees use the smile as a defence mechanism in dangerous situations. But he was a Palestinian and he had seen my book about Israel!

- It is a difficult situation for the Palestinians, I tried, but he didn't answer.

- How do you like the US?

- It's okay, he said and drank some of his coffee with another irritating gulp.

Should I send an SMS to my husband and tell him that I was sitting in a taxi? But I didn't even know where we were, and there was no reason to frighten him if there wasn't any danger. The driver's mobile phone rang. He answered in Arabic and he kept talking for quite a long time. My hands became clammy while I was imagining how he and his Arabic friend were planning to rob me of my money and all my belongings and then just leave me alone at this deserted area. They might even punish me more severely, because of my book about Israel or because I was from Denmark. The cartoon crisis was already some years back in time, but his family and friends might have been burning the Danish flag in protest. I thought about the Danish photographer Jacob Holdt, who had travelled through the worst imaginable surroundings in the US with confidence as his only entrance card.

The lump in my throat grew at the thought of missing my plane home. He hung up and put on some melodious Arabic music, which relieved the tense situation.

- I like the music, I tried, but he didn't answer.

As a revelation, a road sign with O'Hare Airport appeared.

- Which company are you flying with?

- United, I answered.

Ten minutes after he put the brakes on in front of the entrance to the O'Hare airport.

- 95 dollars.

I gave him 110 out of pure relief.

- Have a nice trip! He said with a strong rolling of the 'r' and sent me another mysterious smile.

YIN IN HONG KONG

If anybody had asked me what I liked best after having spent most of the day walking through the Hong Kong neighbourhood of Kowloon, I would have answered the temples and the markets. But let me be honest, the real climax after the exhausting street life and the constant sound of the Chinese and their shrill voices, was to be in a quiet café enjoying a cup of tea with Murakami's novel "Colorless Tsukuru Tazaki and his Years of Pilgrimage", that I had just bought. A quiet and intense drama about the main character's effort to find out why his close friends suddenly, and apparently without any reason, had turned their backs on him.

On my way out of the café, I discovered a small note on the wall saying: *Healthy living in Hong Kong. Yoga lessons, including vinyasa and yin yoga.* I wrote down the address and the phone number and called the place from my hotel room to ask if I could participate in the yin class the next day. A female voice answered in almost unintelligible English: *No ploblem. You ale vely welcome tomollow night!*

The next evening I took the subway from Kowloon to Hong Kong Island and at last I found the yoga studio, which was close to the Man Mo Temple that I had time enough to visit before they closed. The temple was a tribute to the god of literature and war. It was colorfully decorated and big incense sticks were lit for the gods and spreading the spicy aroma to the whole room.

I continued to the yoga studio, which also smelled of some kind of floral aroma. The Chinese woman I had talked to on the phone – I recognized her heavy accent and her replacement of the "r" with an "l" – received me kindly and showed me the changing room and the room, where the yoga class was to be held.

When I entered the yoga room, I saw seven people lying on their yoga mats with their eyes closed. Apparently almost all of them were of Western origin. The yoga teacher, a blonde woman dressed in a black leotard with a cut on the back, which showed a small tattoo between her shoulder blades, received me. "Hi, I am Sheryl, welcome", she whispered, and I immediately recognized her American accent. She showed me an empty mat beside a woman, who was lying with a thick yoga cushion under her shoulder blades, which made her chest shoot up as an arch, while her hands were resting above her head. I lay down and tried to relax.

"Welcome to yin yoga everybody", Sheryl said a while after with a soft voice. She put on some quiet meditation music and asked us to lie down flat on the mat and let all the thoughts that might come just float away like small clouds on the sky. As soon as I had closed my eyes, different thoughts poured through my head. Murakami's novel, remarks that I had got just before leaving for Hong Kong ("Are you travelling again!"... "Isn't your husband going with you?) and many other things. "Just let the sounds you hear be there without paying any attention to them", Sheryl's calm voice said. I did what I could to transform the many thoughts to small clouds, which I tried to throw out into the sky.

After the introductory relaxation, we were asked to sit up and put the right leg in our arms and rock it like a little baby. I was not able to weave my fingers around the leg and squinted at my neighbor, who had pulled her leg all the way to her face and was rocking it with her eyes closed and little smile. The same exercise was repeated with the left leg, and for my part it turned out to be a little more co-operative than the right leg. "There can be a difference between your right and left side", Sheryl commented.

"Now I want you to place yourselves on all fours across the mat and spread your legs to each side like a frog". *The frog pose,* they call this far from comfortable pose in yin yoga. Sheryl said that we could sigh and moan as much as we wanted to, and if we found the pose challenging, we should use deep breathing. At the exhalation, the connective tissues would yield. My neighbour began to sigh very loudly and her breathing in and out was becoming very intense. The sound of her forced and deep sighs had almost driven out all the thoughts that were bustling about in my head, and I felt it as if her deep sighs were increasing the intense tightening in my inner thighs. After three minutes, I heard the welcoming sound of the instructor's little Tibetan clock, which meant that we could get out of the pose and lie on our stomach to relax.

We were asked to come up on our knees again, lean backward and lie down on the yoga cushion behind us. For me this was one of the most infuriating poses in yin yoga. Torture in a light version. My neighbour's rhythmical breathing and sighing now filled the whole room. Suddenly she also began to yawn loudly several times. I looked at Sheryl, but she had her calm expression as if no sounds were heard. I heard a stomach rumble behind me. "This deep stretch of the upper thigh has a strong effect on the meridians of the stomach and in some cases the stomach begins to rumble", Sheryl commented.

The last pose before the final shavasana was the universal stretch, when the lower and the upper body are twisted in opposite directions. My neighbour's deep breathing continued with unabated force. I glanced at her a few times, but she was in a state of deep concentration about her breathing and her eyes were closed.

For the final shavasana Sheryl placed bags on our eyes and gave us a light neck massage. My neighbour's breathing calmed down slowly and was only interrupted by a single "Mmmm", and I guessed that it was her reaction to Sheryl's neck massage. Deep inside me I could still hear her snorting sounds as a remote echo and I tried in vain to transform them into small clouds and just throw them out into the sky.

Shavasana came to an end and Sheryl asked us to get up and sit cross-legged with our eyes closed. With our hands in front of our hearts we ended the yoga class with the mantra OM. We breathed deeply and while exhaling we all chanted OM three times. Once again, I heard my neighbour's deep breathing sounds and her OMs were no less intense. After the class, she gave Sheryl a hug and thanked her for the fantastic class. "I just feel a different person, it really helped!" In the changing room, she noticed me. "Hi, I haven't seen you before! I am Susan". I introduced myself and said that I was on a short visit to Hong Kong and that I was going to Taiwan in a few days. "Oh, I just love Taiwan!" she exclaimed and began to tell me about the Buddhist monastery Fo Guang Shan, which was a must when you visited Taiwan. She told me about the enormous golden statue of Buddha, which had given her such a feeling of peace in her mind that her irritable bowel syndrome almost disappeared. She asked me if I wanted to accompany her to the subway, but I said that I was going to meet someone. She gave me a big hug and wished me a wonderful trip to Taiwan.

When she had left, I went to the nearest bar and asked for a gin and tonic. Double shot, please.

DOVN MEMORY LANE IN LONDON

My husband had often encouraged me to write more short stories about my childhood, but for some reason I couldn't get on with them. One day, however, I decided to show some of the stories I had written to a colleague, who was a teacher of literature. One week later she returned them and said that I had some problems with the angle of the texts and that they required a thorough rewriting. We began to talk about literature in general, and when I enthusiastically mentioned the Danish writer Suzanne Brøgger, she brushed off her books as substandard confessional writing. I asked her if she had read *Don Quixote*. "What a leap from Danish confessional literature to world literature!" she exclaimed and began to talk about the structure of the novel, which raised my suspicion that she had never read the book. However, I am not an opponent of literary analysis; it expands our horizons and gives a greater understanding of other people and their problems. I will even argue that the analysis of a literary work can make us see nuances in our complicated life. But is literature supposed to be used as if it were a branded good like Vuitton or Chanel?

I decided to go for a five-day writing course in London to get some inspiration and I arrived a few days before it began. I had got married to my first husband in London and wanted to see some of the places from those days again. We wanted to rent an apartment in London, but it was impossible at that time without having a marriage certificate. We paid ten shillings each for two witnesses for the ceremony at St Pancras Town Hall. Afterwards we celebrated it at a restaurant and ended at a pub. I had too many Bloody Marys and threw the entire dinner up at the toilet while my new husband was sitting with his pint of bitter talking to a drunk Irishman.

We led a cat-and-dog life in the British capital. Both our respective backgrounds and dreams were too different for us to find a common path with which to walk. But we were both individualists and curious to see the world. However, it took us by surprise that our sudden marriage had now become a family matter. Congratulations cards with drawings of a bride and a groom, she in a white dress, he in a black dinner jacket, poured into our letter box from our families and friends. I could never imagine myself going up the aisle dressed in a white wedding dress, and actually, I just considered the marriage certificate more as an access to some advantages, but not as an evidence of love. Our marriage was at the end of the rebellious 60s, and it hit me when a friend of mine wrote that she was surprised that I had become so conventional as to get married. She got married herself a few years later to a Frenchman, and, after all, maybe I also had hoped to find a French gentleman at heart. I intended to study French in the south of France, but it was my fate to end up in London with a Dane. Even my mother and my grandmother, who were both divorced women, reminded me – taught by bitter experience – that I should consider all options carefully before I decided myself. But it was already too late.

On Trafalgar Square, where the hippies were smoking their hashish at that time, a group of colourful street artists were showcasing their talents at the foot of Lord Nelson and the huge lion sculptures, which are standing there rock-solid witnesses to the changing trends and ideas of time. When I was walking down Oxford Street, my feeling of freedom was much greater than in the middle of the rebellious 60s, when

Jim Morrison intoxicated by drugs was singing "break on through to the other side".

I was on my way to the subway to find the line to Hackney, the dreary neighbourhood where I lived as a newly married, but I changed my mind and went into an Asian restaurant in Soho instead to have some spicy Thai food and a beer. And what was the idea of all this looking back? I had come to London to learn to write.

The next day I arrived at the course in creative writing. We were twelve participants, most of them women. Our tutor Beth had a bobbed and a somewhat masculine hairstyle, which matched well with her straightforward manner. She was an editor of a magazine, which also published short stories. After a short presentation, Beth asked us to do an exercise in automatic writing. We were to write continually for ten minutes about anything that occurred to us, and we were not allowed to think about what we wrote or how we wrote, we should just go on writing.

In spite of her prohibition, I was thinking feverishly about what to write and decided to choose my lost life dreams. The exercise became a fight between my super-ego and my "id". When the "id" appeared with its demonic face, the super-ego turned up to chase away the id.

After ten minutes, Beth asked us to stop and wanted to know if there was anyone who wished to read aloud what they had written aloud. I looked away when I met her eyes. A middle-aged woman volunteered and read about her concern for a terrorist attack on the subway of London. Then Beth asked how each of us had experienced the exercise. I told them about my difficulties with spontaneous writing. It was something I had to work with, to create a flow in my writing process, she concluded. And she even recommended a good therapist who had some fabulous methods to promote spontaneity.

At the end of the course we were asked to write about a memory from our childhood and mail it to Beth. I chose one of the childhood stories that I had written and translated it into English. I played truant one day from my piano lesson, which I hated, and went over to my girl-friend's house. We built a tent of two sheets and in there we took off our pants and played doctor and patient. Suddenly the tent was torn apart and there stood my grandmother looking at us with her severe penetrating eyes.

I made a great effort to follow Beth's advice concerning the use of spontaneity, and when I had finished the story, I felt quite satisfied with the new English version, which seemed almost better than the Danish one.

On the last day of the course, Beth returned our stories with her comments. I quickly looked through the corrections and on the last page I saw her general valuation: WHAT A DISGUST-ING STORY!!!

ARSENIO ARCE

When my translation of an Argentinian novel was published in Denmark, the author's daughter put the cover of the book on Facebook together with a picture of me. Shortly after I got a message from an unknown Argentine man. He introduced himself as the author Arsenio Arce. "I wish there were more people like you", he wrote - whatever he meant by that. Afterwards, I got a friend request on Facebook from the same Arsenio. He hadn't added a picture of himself, but without thinking any further about what this implied, I accepted his request. The same evening, he sent some links to short stories he had published in an Argentinean literary magazine. I was busy packing my suitcase for my trip to Buenos Aires the next day, but as the stories were short, I read them, and I liked one of them in particular, *El sofá* - the sofa. It was about the narrator's relationship to his sofa and about how much he missed it when he was away from home. When he was travelling, he used to visit furniture stores just to be able to sit in a sofa because of his longing for his own sofa. I wrote to him that this was my favourite story, and he immediately answered that he was moved to tears.

The same evening, he had visited my Facebook profile and had looked at all my photos and had chosen some that he found especially nice of me. He also placed a picture of himself on my timeline together with three tango songs by Carlos Gardel. He was cross-eyed and had a bright look that reminded me of a dog looking at a bone that he could not get hold of. I chose not to comment on what he had sent to me.

A few hours later I got three messages from him. "Why hadn't I answered him?" "Was something wrong?", "Did I not like Gardel?" I answered that I was very busy because I was leaving for Buenos Aires the next day and didn't have time for more Facebook now. Good night!

I arrived at Buenos Aires on a sunny morning. It was September and spring was approaching on this side of the globe. I decided to go to the San Telmo neighbourhood to look at the antique market, which I hadn't seen in many years. As the banks were closed, I had to change money at Florida, the main shopping street where several men were shouting: "Cambio, cambio, cambio!" What they made out of changing money on the street, I don't know, but from previous visits to Buenos Aires I didn't have any bad experiences with them and changed a hundred dollars to pesos.

The first thing I caught sight of when I came to San Telmo's famous Plaza Dorrego, was the old tango couple that I had seen at the same corner some twenty years ago. They were around 75, I guessed, and had apparently become fixtures at the Sunday market. There was something comical and almost clownish about them and their dance, which was more theatrical than sensual. The man in his black hat, the lady in a thigh-length skirt, net stockings and high-heeled shoes and her bleached hair put up.

I entered the big indoor market hall to look at the many antique shops. I love dusty antiquities, old furniture in the fin de siècle style, broad-brimmed elegant hats decorated with feathers or flowers, silverware, big hairpins, crystal glasses, stuffed animals, mirrors with twisted frames and grapes on the edges and old paintings. They all aroused my imagination about Buenos Aires at the turn of the century. I pictured the city to myself in its days of prosperity, when it certainly lived up to the designation "Paris of South America". Today you sense the decay everywhere, with faded and run-down rests of the once impressive buildings. To the tones of a slightly cracked edition of Enrique Santos Discépolo's old tango "Yira, yira", which, in a poetic but merciless way expresses that the earth keeps turning without considering all our qualms, I walked around enjoying all the old objects. I was interrupted in the middle of my nostalgic thoughts by my mobile phone - "Hola, it's Arsenio. Welcome to Buenos Aires." I didn't know what to answer, because I thought it was my friend Tamara, whom I was going to meet in the evening. - "Where are you?" – "At Plaza Dorrego", I said and regretted immediately my thoughtlessness. – "I'll be there in half an hour. We can meet at Bar Plaza Dorrego." I hung up without answering. But how had he got my phone number?

I left the antiquity store and began to walk down Calle Defensa, where there is an outdoor market which continues as far as the eye can see. It is a hotchpotch where they sell colourful paintings of tango couples in dramatic poses, pictures of Carlos Gardel, knitwear made of acrylic yarn, old books, tango CDs, containers for *mate*, leather bracelets, etc. Many young couples have seen a possibility to earn some extra money by dancing the tango for the crowds of tourists that gather on this market. In tourist areas people seem to accept anything, as long as it's tango. The choreography can often be too dramatic, with too many rapid leg movements for my taste, even though I always find it quite amusing to observe the many expressions this dance offers.

The telephone rang again. It was Arsenio's number. I didn't answer, but considered taking a taxi and going somewhere else. But should this pushy guy be allowed to tyrannize all my movements? I continued my walk down the long row of stalls with cheap rubbish. There was something about these sellers that I didn't like. Was it their tattoos, their piercings and the hairstyles with half their head shaved and a tuft of hair left on top, which contributed to accentuate their hardened expressions?

In the middle of the crowd I caught sight of a man with a look that reminded me of Arsenio's hungry dog eyes. I quickly looked the other way, put my sunglasses on and pushed through the crowd without looking back. I chose to leave the market and moved to some less busy streets, where the atmosphere corresponded to my conceptions of the neighbourhoods where the tango flourished in the 30s with paved streets and old street lamps between the trees. The old tangos that give the cruelty of life a poetic expression. I heard the sound of an SMS in my bag. "You didn't answer. Is something wrong? Maybe you are suffering from jetlag after the long flight. I am waiting for you at Bar Dorrego. Arsenio". I sat down on a bench and answered: "Leave me alone. I don't want to see you". The telephone rang shortly after and I turned it off.

I took a taxi back to my hotel. On my way back, I asked the driver about the new government. "There is no difference. They are all the same. Equally corrupt the lot. They put everything in their own pockets, and then we are the ones who have to pay the bill", was his conclusion. When I was to pay the 80 pesos it cost and gave him a bill of 100 pesos, he looked at it and said that it wasn't okay. "It's an old note and they won't do anymore. You have to use the new notes. Can I see what you have in your purse? You can give me some dollars instead," he hissed, and his cheerful face turned grim and hard. "I don't have any dollars with me," I lied. "Then show me what you have", he commanded with quite an unpleasant look. I picked some of the old 100 pesos notes and one 50 peso notes up. He pointed at the 50 peso notes. "That's one of the new bills. Don't you have any more of those?" I came to think of the 100 dollars I had changed at Calle Florida. Had they cheated me? I

186

gave him the 50 pesos note and the old 100 peso notes and said that I didn't have anything else to offer him, because I didn't know that the old notes were not in use anymore. Then I hurried out of the car and went straight to the hotel without even looking at the driver. I asked the receptionist if the old 100 pesos notes were not in use anymore. "Oh yes, they still are in use", she assured me. The driver's look was still on my retina while I went up in the elevator. Damned Mafiosos! Up in my room I took out my computer and deleted Arsenio from my facebook friend list.

The next day, when I went to the department of Argentine literature at the bookstore Ateneo, I caught sight of three books by Arsenio Arce. *El sofá y otros cuentos* – "The sofa and other stories" was the title of one of them. I looked at the back of the book and there I once again saw the same squinting dog eyes as on the Facebook-photo, which had landed on my timeline. "*Arsenio Arce has achieved a totally personal style. A dominant theme in his characteristic and poetic stories is the aberration and his search for a fixed point in life*".

A TABLE FOR ONE

1.

It was my first visit to Buenos Aires and one of my preferred sights was Parque Lezama, the location where Ernesto Sábato's novel *On Heroes and Tombs* begins. I was sitting on a bench beside the statue of the goddess Ceres with the beginning of Sábato's novel in mind: *On a Saturday in May, 1953, two years before the events in Barracas, a tall, stoop-shouldered youngster was walking along one of the footpaths in the Parque Lezama. He sat down on a bench, near the statue of Ceres, and remained there, doing nothing, lost in thought.*

Exhilarated by the surroundings, I chose to eat lunch afterwards at a restaurant with a view to the park. It was jam packed with people who were having their Sunday lunch, and the chatter was ringing out in the room, which was furnished in a rustic style and with a lit fireplace.

- Do you have a table for one person? I asked the waiter.

- Of course! ... Only for you? He asked wonderingly.

- Yes... I am from Denmark and this is my first visit to Buenos Aires.

- *Dinamarca!* He exclaimed enthusiastically and arranged a small table for me.

- You have to try an *asado*, the Argentine barbecue.

- But I am a vegetarian!

- And you must have a glass of good Malbec wine.

He was already on his way out to the kitchen and in his eagerness he forgot all about my vegetarianism. Fifteen minutes after he returned beaming with joy with an enormous piece of barbecued beef and a glass of Malbec. While I grudgingly put my teeth into the meat, some children were running around between the tables, while their parents, grandparents, aunts and uncles were engaged in lively discussions. A family life I envied them. When I asked for the bill, the waiter was just dying to hear my opinion about the *asado* and the Malbec.

- *Fantástico!* The Argentines make wonderful food and wine, but I couldn't eat all the French fries. The dish was very big.

I paid my bill and hurried out before he discovered that I had hidden half of the beef under the French fries and covered it with my napkin.

2.

Café Richmond in Buenos Aires was originally a meeting place for famous Argentine men of letters with Jorge Luis Borges in the lead. I had been looking forward to seeing the café for a long time and glanced at the interior through the window to reconnoiter. The furnishings seemed very British with leather-covered chairs, big mirrors on the walls and beautiful panels of oak and waiters of the classic style that hardly exist anymore. I entered and asked for a table for one person. The waiter, who reminded me of an English butler, took my coat and showed me a small table for two.

- I can recommend *negroni con ingredientes*. It's one of our specialities, he said, and I accepted the proposal.

Most of the guests were single men, who were reading the newspaper, and an elderly couple who seemed to be bored. The man was reading a paper whilst his wife looked around the room with displeasure. Why doesn't she also read a book or a newspaper?

The waiter came with a big tray filled with small bowls with cold and warm snacks, sausages, ham, olives, pâtés and cheese and a glass of with the cocktail negroni. There was enough for two people.

When I was about to eat, I discovered that one of the men reading was observing me with an intense look. He looked attractive, as many of the elderly Argentinian men do, with his gray brushed back-hair that was a little longer at the neck. I tried to ignore it and began to eat some of the tempting *ingredientes*. Once in a while I cast a sidelong glance at the man with his paper, and each time he caught my eye like an animal lying in wait for its prey. I tried to avoid direct eye contact and began to read a book. The awareness of being observed had the effect that I didn't pick up on one word of the text. After five or ten minutes, I once again glanced at him and his eyes hit me like a bolt of lightning. The blood rushed to my cheeks and I looked to the other side. I took a big drop of my negroni and kept looking to the other side. The next time I glanced at him, I discovered that he was about to pay. He put on his hat and walked slowly to the entrance, where he put on his dark blue coat, and without as much as deigning to look at me, he went out. He stood for a short while in the street, cast a glance at the café and left. I don't know if he had seen that I had looked at him. When I could finally enjoy my food and the peace and quiet, everything seemed so empty.

That night I had an erotic dream about the Argentine gentleman in the café. In the dream, he succeeded in seducing me.

Many years later, when I wanted to relive Café Richmond, I discovered that this café so rich in tradition, and even was put on UNESCO's World Heritage List, had been shut down and replaced by a Nike shop – exactly like the distinguished Café A'Porta in the heart of Copenhagen, which has been replaced by Mc Donald's.

3.

The entire centre of Salta, which lies in a valley in the Andes some 1000 meters above sea level, is characterised by the Spanish colonial style. In contrast to the rest of Argentina, where the population are descendants of European immigrants from Italy, Spain and Russia, a major part of Salta's inhabitants are descendants of Indians.

It was lunchtime and I was looking for a restaurant without a tourist menu and waiters dressed in black hats, white shirts, black plus fours and black boots. I found a place with rustic furnishing, where the walls were decorated with different riding gear, saddles, spurs, whips, leather boots and big woven carpets in lively colours. The menu consisted of local stews with pumpkins, beans and maize. Without hesitating, the waiter showed me to a table close to another unaccompanied woman, who was reading a novel with a French title. Her expression was very tense, and even when her food was served, she didn't give up her reading, but turned over its pages with hectic movements. She did, in any case, not need company. I also began to read my book about Evita Perón, while I was waiting for my food.

When the waiter came with my empanadas, he looked at the title of my book.

- Evita did so much for Argentina! He exclaimed enthusiastically.

- Wasn't she also a tyrannical woman?

- No! She was not!... There are so many lies in circulation about Evita and very likely also in your book... Evita did so much for the poor...

- At the Evita museum in Buenos Aires they display all her gala dresses, among other things from Dior, and hats worth fortunes... She was also known to be vain...

A dark curtain was pulled down over the waiter's cheerful face.

- She was a saint...

The woman with the French book looked up for a moment, but quickly returned to her frantic

196

reading. I abstained from commenting upon the remark. The previously kind waiter came with my main course and placed it on the table without even smiling.

I asked for the bill, which was given to me without a word. In return, I placed the exact amount on the table, but without so much as a penny as a tip.

4.

At a small Hindu restaurant in London the waiter apparently took a similar view as his colleague in Salta. Single women should sit next to each other.

The restaurant was decorated with big bronze figures of the Hindu elephant god Ganesh and the dancing Shiva. Even though there were many other free tables, he showed me to a table next to a single woman, who looked just as Nordic as I did. She immediately said hello and curiously asked where I came from. "From Denmark." She brightened up. "I am from Holland. My name is Anneke."

While I studied the menu and enjoyed the tones of the slow raga, I could feel her eagerness in getting into contact with me. After having ordered, I took up a newspaper from my bag and began to read.

When the waiter came with my food, she seized the opportunity.

- I came to London with my girlfriend, but she became ill and is now in a hospital, and my vacation is totally spoiled...

- But there are so many museums and other interesting sights in London, I tried in an aloof tone of voice and put the fork in one of the Bombay potatoes.

- Maybe we could walk around together, she suggested.

- I have an appointment with some friends for the next few days - it slipped out of me, and I could see the disappointment on her face.

As soon as I had finished eating, I asked for the bill and said that I was in a hurry, because I had to meet my friends.

While I was walking towards the nearest subway, Anneke's disappointed expression came up at regular intervals, and even if I tried to distract myself, I couldn't escape her imploring eyes.

5.

At one of the beautiful plazas in Cádiz I found a restaurant, which seemed so attractive with its yellow tablecloths and blue tiles on the walls. The tables were filled with families and groups of people, and the lively sound of the talking guests echoed in the room. I waited for quite a while, but the waiters didn't even look at me, and I ended up by approaching one of them to ask if there was a table for me. He looked wonderingly and took me to a table in a dull out-of-the-way corner.

- But there is a small table over there, I objected.

- It is already booked, he said, but I didn't believe him.

It required several hints and gestures before I got my menu. Were the waiters a bunch of old Franco devotees, who found it improper to have single women in a restaurant? Long after the death of the Spanish dictator you could still see slogans like "Under Franco everything was better". When I had finished my meal and paid, I chose not to give a tip. Beside my glass, I placed a small note with the following text: *If this restaurant finds it improper to have single women at the tables, I recommend you to put a sign at the entrance saying NO ENTRY TO SINGLE WOMEN.*

6.

In a small provincial town in South India I had to wait almost half a day before I could continue my trip by train to Madras. I walked around

199

with my suitcase and everywhere people were staring at me quite unrestrainedly. A flock of children followed me and I could hear them laughing behind me. Each time I turned around, I saw their small dark heads and roguish eyes quickly disappear behind the corner.

Finally, I found a small restaurant. A very friendly waiter asked me to take a seat on the straw mat on the ground, where I sat like a yogi with my legs crossed. Three other waiters came in and began to bustle about me with glasses, spoon and fork etc., which they placed on a piece of cloth in front of me. The only waiter who spoke English said with his characteristic Hindu accent, that I should try a *tali*. While I was waiting for the food, another waiter, who was standing a little further away, kept an eye on me. A third waiter came in and placed a big napkin on my knees, and finally my *tali* came in. Ten small bowls with all kinds of delicacies were served on a banana-leaf. I didn't know what the food consisted of apart from a bowl with Bombay potatoes. The English-speaking waiter gave me the Indian names of the small dishes and told me about the ingredients, which I had never heard of, and in which order they should be eaten. When I began to eat, the waiters stood in a circle around me and followed each of my movements with a smile. I enjoyed the different taste nuances of spices, but if I took twice from one bowl, they immediately objected and reminded me of the order. I should also try the next dish with the bread. The order had to be kept. For this superb lunch I only paid about one pound and I was satisfied for the rest of the day after such a feast.

7.

A somewhat different atmosphere met me at the restaurant of the legendary Hotel Taj Mahal in Bombay, built in the colonial era. Here the waiter hardly raised his eyebrows when I asked for a table for one person. He showed me a small table at the window and handed me the menu with an almost arrogant coolness, which he probably had learned after having served one Croesus more demanding after the other. In this snotty atmosphere I could at least eat my food in peace without having a lot of waiters bustling around me. Beside my table sat a British couple, who were having their afternoon-tea with scones and biscuits. The wife was looking at the room with her stiff upper-lip, while her husband, dressed in shorts, was reading his newspaper. A little further away two Indian businessmen dressed in light lounge suits filled the whole room with their loud voices. Beside them two Americans in shorts, t-shirts and sneakers, which contrasted with the elegant surroundings, had spread out a map of India on the table. They were discussing all the places they had seen and were going to visit: Taj Mahal, Elephanta Caves, Goa, etc.

My cup of tea and a small sandwich cost about four times as much as the fantastic *tali* in the South Indian village, but to be able to sit undisturbed was worth the price.

8.

On a cold spring day, I stepped on the red carpet of Le Train Bleu in Paris. With almost regal feelings I entered this unique belle époque interior just beside the railway station Gare de Lyon.

The restaurant was inaugurated in 1900 on the occasion of the World Exhibition in Paris. A polite and bowing waiter showed me into the salon where the walls and the ceilings were decorated with 41 landscape paintings from the route Paris-Lyon-Mediterranée girdled with golden cherubs and vines.

Even if vegetarianism isn't considered to be in the highest echelons of French gastronomy, I succeeded *sans problèmes* in obtaining an exquisite vegetarian menu made with both artistry and sophistication. I was enjoying my first course, a beautiful green pea soup with a small lump of whipped cream on top, when a conspicuous couple entered the room. An elderly woman dressed in a dark purple turban, which matched her long dress in the same colour. She was about 75, I guessed, or more.

Her companion was probably her son and in all probability a rich manager or businessman. He was an attractive man whose cultivated manners were worthy of a professor. I had a feeling of a man who was fond of women. Maybe it was his look, his smile or something else, that gave me the associations of a cultured Casanova. The waiter served them with a congenial politeness, which revealed them as regular customers of this restaurant, maybe especially the man, who got an extra bow each time he asked for something. Perhaps he frequented the restaurant quite often with other women. That's the kind of secret waiters at well-reputed restaurants keep and never reveal. My main course, a sophisticated vegetable tart decorated with fresh mint leaves and a clear red sauce, was served and presented. While the elderly woman with the turban was studying the menu, I saw that Casanova had turned his eyes towards me and sent me this almost imperceptible smile. Somewhat flustered, I also sent him an imperceptible smile and drank some wine, while he also tasted his champagne. It was as if we both had touched glasses with each other.

Once they had ordered, they sat talking intimately to each other. I was just about to drink my coffee, when the courteous Casanova got up and slowly walked towards the bathroom. A minute after the waiter came with a small tray with a glass of liqueur. "The gentleman who sits over there wants to invite you for a glass of *poire*", the waiter said with a discrete smile. When Casanova returned to his seat, he raised his glass and sent me a smile, this time a little less discreet, and I felt that I had to do the same. I had no idea whether his mother had discovered his games. She had opened a small compact and was powdering her nose.

I paid my bill and slowly passed their table as if nothing had happened.

PARIS REVISITED

One night, when I was a bit depressed, I began to read the book "Baal Babilonia" by the Spanish author Fernando Arrabal and became so absorbed by it that I read the entire volume in one go. It was in the beginning of my life together with Sten, who during most of our first year together had repeatedly urged me to read this book.

Arrabal is one of the few surviving artists in exile of the group that came to Paris in the beginning of the 20th century, among others Samuel Beckett and Eugène Ionesco. Like Arrabal, many of them came from totalitarian regimes, where they couldn't express themselves freely. In the liberal Parisian spirit, however, they flourished and found an outlet for their ideas and fantasies.

"Baal Babilonia" became the beginning of my acquaintance with Arrabal, who has given me occasion to visit Paris several times, where he has lived since 1954 in a self-imposed exile. My last visit to the French capital was in 2012 on the occasion of Arrabal's 80th birthday.

This time I did not arrive in a couchette, but rather by plane at Charles de Gaulle. I stayed at a small hotel in the Marais and began my walking tour in this beautiful neighbourhood with buildings that have accommodated the French nobility and the Jewish society around Rue des Rosiers with its kosher shops and restaurants. I hadn't visited Paris for many years and therefore enjoyed my walk to the full.

I went on to Ile St. Louis, the quiet island with a view of which I can never get enough to the Seine and Notre Dame in the background and the beautiful sand coloured buildings. I continued to Boulevard Saint Michel, which now just seemed to be a shopping-street like so many others. On my way down from Montmartre I met a drunk Finn, who raised his beer bottle and shouted "kippis" to me. If it were my high cheekbones that revealed my Finnish origin or just some drunken nonsense, I don't know.

Arrabal's birthday party was celebrated at the studio of one of his artist friends. Instead of bringing a gift, all the invited guests were asked to perform for the author. My contribution was an anecdote about my first meeting with Arrabal.

I came to Paris in 1984 to conduct an interview with Arrabal in preparation for a textbook about him that I was preparing. Each morning before the interview I repeated my question to this, according to the international press, scandal-ridden author. I was especially interested in his childhood in Spain during the Franco regime, which he describes in such a moving way in Baal Babilonia. The evening before the interview I visited the legendary tango café Trottoirs de Buenos Aires to listen to Argentinian tango music. The same night I dreamt about the upcoming meeting with Arrabal. He was sitting in a huge white sofa and was extremely small. His feet were like a baby's. I sat in front of him with my tape recorder, but suddenly I came to a standstill and didn't know what to ask him.

With butterflies in my stomach, I got off the metro at the Wagram station in the 17th arrondisement and walked to rue Jouffroy. I rang the doorbell, and a woman's voice asked me to take the elevator up to the third floor. I entered a big staircase and took the elevator. When I stepped out, the first thing that I saw was an enormous picture of a knight in a medieval armour à la Don Quixote beside the entrance door. A maid opened the door for me and said that monsieur Arrabal would receive me in a few minutes. She showed me to a big room, where I stood surrounded by macabre and surrealistic paintings, which almost all depicted the author himself in different roles, one of them with the title "Arrabal saved by Fenix" — on which a large eagle-like bird flew with Arrabal in its beak, or a nude picture of Arrabal and his wife Luce, in which their bodies and genders were mixed up.

While I was staring at a painting, where Generalísimo Franco accompanied by Hitler and Mussolini were placing a couple of enormous forceps on the breast of a nude woman, who was tied to a pole, my imaginings about the author, whom I was about to meet, became more and more diabolic. A sudden impulse to run away occurred to me, when a creak behind me pulled me away from my thoughts. Like a magician, a dishevelled man with drowsy eyes and tousled hair appeared in the doorway.

- I fell asleep and had forgotten all about our meeting, he said, and asked if I wanted to smoke an authentic Havana cigar.

He was wearing black patent leather shoes, but he had forgotten to put socks on, and a small amount of bare skin stood in a comical contrast to the shining shoes. We entered his study, where the books lay in piles on the floor. I turned on the tape recorder, but the interview is a communication form, with which I have never been able to come to terms. The thought of putting a number of stereotypical questions that he, without doubt, had heard ad nauseam, brought me to a standstill. Arrabal took out a bottle of calvados from his cupboard and served me one glass after the other while he played a record of the Danish children's song "Ekkoleg", the signature tune of his film "Viva la muerte". He told me that he had found it in a shop in Copenhagen while he was trying to find some pornographic magazines. The inciting melody tore me out of my paralysis and reminded me of the many violent scenes in the film, which is a symbolical description of Arrabal's traumatic childhood-experiences in Franco's Spain. Our conversation became natural.

- Your father was a victim of the Fascists. Have you identified yourself with him?... Because you were also a prisoner of Franco because of your blasphemous statement...

- Yes, he was the model. A mythical model. The best thing a father can do for his children is to disappear. My father gave me the possibility to create a myth, and that was the gift. The myth was his gift.

Through the half-open door, I saw a glimpse of a young woman in a long black dress slide by like a revelation. I guessed that it was his daughter.

- But if I am somebody today, it is because of the women in my life, not only my mother, but also my aunt, my grandmother and my wife. I think that my mother has played the role as a consecrate in my life, he added.

Not until later, I read Arrabal's book "La pierre de la folie" (The Stone of Madness) and understood the deeper meaning of this role. The narrator is confront-

211

ed with his Anima, the female personification of sub-consciousness of a man, which originates in his mother. In the dreamlike atmosphere of the book she appears in different investments, among other things, as a grotesque vampire. At last the opposition between mother and son is dissolved, and the narrator returns to his mother's womb to be reborn. The positive function of Anima as the figure who consecrates the man into a deeper insight about himself and the mysteries of the universe come into force.

The day after the birthday party I walked along the Seine and passed Notre Dame. A sign outside said that there would be a concert in a few moments. Bach's Toccata and Fuga in D minor. I entered and found a free seat beside a small woman dressed in black, who was sleeping with folded hands. The church was crowded to bursting-point. The old woman's face was wrinkled and her hands were bony. While I was admiring the beautiful rosette windows, the organ began to play in a deep tone that increased in power and waved through the enormous church interior. I looked at the old woman beside me. She was totally immovable, and her face seemed so pale. Was she alive? Suddenly I felt as if the organ music was lifting the whole church interior up towards the sky. It was as if we were floating in step with the roaring music. The old woman had opened her eyes. She looked towards the high Gothic vaults, and her eyes were filled with thankfulness.